Fair Game

Fair Game

A Comedy of Regency Manners

Daisy Vivian

Walker and Company
New York

First published in the United States of America in 1986 by the Walker
Publishing Company, Inc.

Published simultaneously in Canada by John Wiley & Sons
Canada, Limited, Rexdale, Ontario.

Library of Congress Cataloging-in-Publication Data

Vivian, Daisy.
    Fair game.

    I. Title.
PS3572.I86F35 1986   813'.54   85-15336
ISBN 0-8027-0860-9

Printed in the United States of America

10 9 8 7 6 5 4 3 2 1

For my sister,
Meredith Lee Grdinich

1

LEGAL MATTERS PERTAINING to the manor of Pentreath had been in the hands of Witherings—father, son, and grandson—for generations. After the horrendous conflagration which destroyed the great house, it was to 'Young' Withering that fell the task of sorting out. This gentleman was referred to as I have done throughout the breadth of Penwith, but the fact is that he was well past his first youth. He was a substantial person of full maturity and no little fortune, the law being what it is, and was experienced and capable in his profession. Nevertheless, the task which faced him was a melancholy one.

Gazing about him now, he found that this parlour of Lady Augusta Mabyn's house in St. Buryan was much as he remembered it from years past: the same Porthminster carpet in soft grey, moss green and rose, the same delicate, rather old-fashioned furniture glowing with evidence of loving care. Only the draped curtains at the window were new, and a small clock on the mantel. There had been a time when, setting his cap for the earl's youngest daughter, he had thought perhaps to reside herein. Such a marriage would have been suitable enough, even from a dynastic perspective, for the Witherings were old stock and as well off financially as the Pentreaths had ever been. But the moment had come and gone, the notion lost, and the lady in question married to another, far *less* suitable, husband, however briefly. Young Withering was not sure, after all these years, exactly how he had felt about it at the time . . . or even exactly how it had happened. Had the decision to draw back been his or the lady's? Perhaps each had been somewhat shy of a match. Or was it that the old earl had, at the last, fancied a finer prospect? If such were the case, he had been doomed to disappointment, for in the end her ladyship had run off to Paris with a poet, of all things. For many years after her sudden widowhood she had reigned as the chatelaine of Pentreath, her brother's wife having, thoughtlessly, passed on. But here in this parlour, time had failed in its flight: moss rose, moss green, subdued, comfortable, and genteel. It was a very pleasant return and presently he was balancing a cup of bohea and discussing certain documents with his client.

"There have been great inroads upon the estate, as you know."

"I know," she replied softly.

"I fear your brother could not support both his sad . . . proclivities . . . and still put the necessary money back into the land."

"Yes," she agreed.

"It seems to be a kind of sickness in some . . . a mania, if you will."

Lady Augusta clucked impatiently. "Oh, tush, sir, pray stop beating about the bush. My brother Radclyffe could not escape the lure of the tables and he was a demmed poor player. Even I had more bottom in that respect than my brother. I am sure that whatever profit he drew from the Pentreath estates went into the capacious pockets of his cronies . . . and the shipping revenues, too, when he had 'em!"

Young Withering nodded sadly. "After the loss of *The Indian Queen* off Malabar, he was forced to mortgage for capital. Always a mistake, in my view." He coughed lightly. "You understand that it was contrary to my own advice, but . . ." he spread his hands deprecatingly ". . . the Earl made his own mind."

Lady Augusta rose from her chair and moved aimlessly about the room. On the brink of forty, she was a strikingly handsome woman still, though pale and somewhat distraught at the moment. The manor house of Pentreath had been her home for a good portion of her life, all her roots were there. Pentreath ancestors had built it as an Elisabethan farmhouse and subsequent inheritors had furbished it in the taste of their own time, adding and subtracting until the very walls were as much a part of the family as the portraits which hung upon them or the inhabitants who lived within them. Now it was all gone, the walls, the portraits, the roots, and, she was discovering, gone were the funds which could have given foundation for a new Pentreath, or even provided dowries for her two nieces. It was hard to believe that her brother had been so in the grip of his gambling fever that he threw away even the futures of his children.

"I am certain you have done your best with his affairs, Mr. Withering. No blame can possibly fall to you on that score. I suppose," she asked somewhat wistfully, "that there is no use thinking of *The Grand Moghul*? She was never officially declared lost, I believe?"

Withering was genuinely distressed. "I fear nothing will come of that, dear lady. Eventually there will be insurance money, of course, but it will be largely eaten up by the earl's debts." He brighten. "You still retain *your* legacy, of course, since it comes from your mother's family. You and the girls—the young ladies, I should say—might live very nicely on that here in St. Buryan, or even in Penzance. Eight hundred a year, after all, is not inconsiderable."

Her ladyship concurred in a resigned fashion. "It would do nicely enough if they were content to live the sort of second-remove life their aunt has done." She gave a sort of wryly ironic smile. "Hardly, though, what Radclyffe had meant for his daughters, or what I had envisioned for them."

Young Withering tutted. "I am sure you would find that it is possible to make very good marriages for them right here in the county."

"I had hoped not to settle for merely *good*. Lavinia is now, after all, a countess in her own right, and a beauty like Barbara can hardly be thrown away on a clerk or a farmer." She paused, stricken. "Oh, dear Mr. Withering, I meant no offense. Your suit to me was a great honour. If I had accepted it I know I should not be in the straits I find myself."

The lawyer reassured her. "Water under the bridge, my dear. I am happy that we came back to being friends after it all."

"Yes, we have, have we not? And I am grateful for your friendship.

"Nevertheless," she repeated, "I had hoped that they must not merely settle for *good*. There must be some suitable alliance, if only we can find it. The Pentreath antecedants, after all, are not inconsiderable. Even after Radclyffe's demise and the shocking state of affairs began to be known, I had thought we still should have the house as crown to the land, and that we should somehow manage for them, perhaps with my own money. But now . . . ." Fingers to temples she stared sightlessly out of the window. "The present insurance money would provide for one moderately brilliant comeout, but, even at best, it could not do for two so awkwardly placed apart."

"The young ladies cannot share the occasion?"

"They could but for the bemusements of time. Barbara will not properly be ready for another year and Lavinia, by rights, should have been introduced a year ago. She would have been, of course, but for her papa's untimely demise."

Young Withering's brow was wrinkled in thought. "You certainly must not think of using the legacy from your mother, since that and the little income you yourself derive from Pentreath are all you have. Thank God nothing can touch that. Is there none among your family connexion who would come to your aid in this—some female relative who would share a ball between her daughter and your nieces?"

Lady Augusta laughed shortly. "You must be mad! A mother who would consent to sharing her darling's debut with the likes of Barbara? I fear you have no understanding of women, sir. It is generally considered a disadvantage to be *too* great a beauty. I fear that poor Barbara will come to know that all too well. The hard facts are that both money and prospects are in deucedly short supply."

"Do you not have a cousin? Lady Mawson?"

Unladylike though it was, Augusta Mabyn all but hooted with laughter. "Cousin Christabel? As plain as her gels are? There may be somewhere a fashion to be generous, but country families are a little selfish with their kin when a great advantage is to be taken from it. The Lady Christabel would not lift a finger, I assure you, nor would I demean myself by courting her certain refusal."

"And there are no friends?"

Lady Augusta opened, then closed her fan with a sharp snap of impatience. "Am I reduced to begging, then? It comes home now that I have always found the company of my own sex to be too silly and trivial to be borne. I should have looked to the future, I suppose, but, alas, I have always been (as you above others are aware) remarkably self-sufficient."

Young Withering's grimace was partly one of amusement, but more of chagrin. "Yes, I am aware of that, your ladyship. But, reverting to the subject of economy . . . I know little of such things, but would not the new Assembly Room in Chapel Street suggest certain opportunities?"

"The Assembly Room? You astonish me! Here am I prattling of a London season and you offer me the Assembly Room. As it happens, the *new* Assembly Room, as you call it, is a good ten years old and was already remarkably shabby after five. I have already said that I do not wish to settle for *good*, and what would my girls meet there but what passes for society in Cornwall . . . farmers, petty gentry, and men of the professions. All the best of the region, I grant you, but must we, because we love Cornwall think it a part of the great world? No Cornishman of my acquaintance does, I assure you, and prefers not to. Penzance is *not* London, by wish of Cornishman and Londoner alike."

"Well, Truro, then," suggested Withering, "or Plymouth if you feel it necessary to have a larger canvas on which to limn. Since, as I hear it, you have one title and one raving beauty, cannot each stand for the other?"

Lady Augusta sighed. "They could if the ages were reversed,

or even if we stretched a point and brought them out together, but none of that alters the geography. It is quite true that Barbara is, as the new fashion has it, a 'stunner', but she requires a proper setting. And, you know, there are certain unfortunate equities at play."

"Indeed?" asked the lawyer. "You are saying . . .?"

· Lady Augusta hesitated. Her affection for her younger niece was as great as that for Countess Lavinia and she did not wish to appear disloyal to either. She hoped that Jonathan Withering, in the way of an old friend, would take her meaning.

"Barbara is very beautiful and very much sought after, but she is not . . . not *clever*. I do not mean to say that she is simple, you know, but that God has so arranged the shares so that she has the beauty and Lavinia the intelligence."

"*And* the title," Withering added. "Hardly a matter for commiseration, I should say, and I wonder that you should speak so of her ladyship. As I recall she is a handsome enough young creature in her own right."

His hostess chuckled at the way he had caught her up. "Heavens, I see that I have misspoke, after all, and I did not think I could do that with you." She tapped him coquettishly upon the knee with her Hondouras fan and he remembered how high-spirited, almost racy, a girl she had been.

"I do not mean to imply that it is all sharp-cut. Lavvy would be well enough if she would put herself in the way of it, but she will not. She prides herself on sheer common sense and has no patience with what she calls fal-lals. I daresay she would be a Puritan if she could, or some other kind of dissenter. Certainly she would liefer be out on the moors with the grouse and foxes than in any *proper* company. It is always either that, or losing her head in a book.

"As for that, Barbara is well enough in conversation. I do not mean to present them as a ninny and a drab, but they do not pull well together, being so unlike." She drifted aimlessly toward the window and stood there silhouetted against the afternoon light. "My poor, penniless girls."

Young Withering, reverting for the moment to his old sense

of familiarity in this sitting-room, poured himself another cup of tea. It proved to be cooler than he liked it and he was tempted to ring for more, but restrained the impulse. Time enough for that. Instead, he began to think out loud, counting on his fingers.

"By my calculations, the Lady Barbara is nearly seventeen years of age. I can see what you mean, that is an awkward time. In these days still a child, but in the past well beyond the age of betrothal."

"One of our ancestresses gave birth to her first son at the ripe age of fourteen," said Lady Augusta, "but that was considered extreme, even then." She came back to the tea-table. "But Barbara must have a lord, it would be so awkward otherwise."

"I must say," offered the lawyer after having sugared his tea lavishly, sipped it, then put it down, "if you will forgive me my bluntness, I fear you will find you have set your sights rather impossibly high. Great alliances such as you envision are not made dowryless.

"Although," he hastened to add, "the young ladies may *not* be without funds. We shall not be sure of that until the insurance is figured in. In any case, your ladyship has, in fact, no true responsibility for their welfare, since your legacy is your own and does not enter into the question."

Lady Augusta looked at him as if he had taken leave of his senses. "No responsibility, sir? What an absurdity! They are my family, if you please, and we will hear no more such silliness on *that* note." Then she softened. "What *shall* I do, old friend?"

The lawyer licked his lips meditatively. "I know you will not regard it, but the answer, your ladyship, is to live as quietly as possible. Who can tell? If you begin to extend your circle of influence by degrees, you may soon find that St. Buryan here becomes the centre of Penwith, Penwith the centre of Cornwall, metaphorically speaking, Cornwall of Britain and, since our navy rules the world, you might find yourself, you know, the monarch of all!"

"Oh, gammon! Bottle your fancy. Shall I tell you what I have in mind to do? I must gamble, what say you to that?"

"On *your* income, madame, it is madness! No prudent man would ever advise such a measure. Look at the number of people who have been ruined. Look, if you will, at the Duchess of Devonshire, who has become a national scandal with her play at the tables."

"As for that," smiled Lady Augusta, "if I had Georgiana's fortune, this conversation would be unnecessary. But, no, I had in mind something more professional than playing badly for social reasons. I am thinking of opening a club."

"What, a gambling club?"

"Yes, I had thought to have card-playing."

The lawyer was aghast. His mouth all but fell open. "Have you had a seizure of the brain, madam? I hope you will do no such thing!"

"And I cannot count on you?"

"I have a reputation, ma'am, that was not built on such means as that."

"You dismay me. I had thought you had more spirit," said her ladyship rather tartly. "You do not even listen."

"If you want support for such views as that, Lady Augusta, you must seek other ears to hear them. I daresay the Mad Vicar would take your part, grand gestures being quite his style."

"The Vicar cannot give me sensible monetary advice." Good humour was restored. "I must depend upon you for that. Will you not hear me?"

The lawyer shook his head sadly as if he were used to this sort of ploy. "Very well. I have no objection to listening, but . . ." he raised a cautionary finger ". . . listening only, mind you. I represent a blank wall upon which to throw your mind."

"I trust I shall not sink to becoming a *camera obscura*. What I have in mind is this."

She dropped her voice confidentially although they were alone in the room. The lawyer listened, his eyebrows slightly arched in expressive toleration, but as she continued the arches became more and more pronounced, the faintly sleepy eyes widened in astonishment, the narrow mouth opened and paused midway between outrage and incredulity. When her ladyship

14

had done, Withering leaned back in his chair as if exhausted and took a deep breath to replenish that which had been knocked out of him by the disclosure of her intentions; then, as quickly, he bobbed forward again as if he could not believe the fantasy he had just heard.

"Bless my blood, madam, I cannot decide whether you are quizzing me or if you are serious, and, if you *are* serious, if you have not been driven out of your head by grief. And you talk to *me* of absurdity! You'd never pull it off, and you would, into the bargain, ruin any chances the young ladies might have in society! Better they should marry among the admittedly minor gentry of Cornwall than be exposed to wickedness and ruin."

"Will you wager on my success, or are you too hidebound for even a friendly fling?"

"I see you know all the cant, but there is more to this than language, madam. I beg you to think again." Impulsively he grasped her hand. "Do me the justice of reconsidering. Examine my point of view."

She agreed reluctantly. "Well, I will ponder it a little more, but only because we are old friends and I know your excessive caution springs from your care for me."

Withering took this as a triumph of masculine reason. Smiled broadly, he delicately tapped the side of the teapot. "I say, do you suppose we might have fresh tea?"

Even as he spoke Branston entered with a fresh kettle. "I wondered if this might not be required, madam," he announced.

"O, excellent Branston," crowed the guest. "What a treasure you are! I hope you will come into my employ one day if only as an example to the other servants."

The butler acknowledged this muted offering with a smug look of forbearance, and Lady Augusta felt it necessary to emphasise her dominance. "I believe we are expecting another guest," she reminded him.

"Yes, madam. Cook has made scones especially for the Vicar since she knows how partial he is to them."

"Here!" Withering objected. "Do you mean to say I have teacakes foisted off on me and the Mad Vicar is to be orgified with scones? I say unfair, Lady Augusta! With currants, too, I'll wager."

"Sultanas, actually, sir." Branston smiled.

The lawyer shook his head sadly. "Worse and worse."

"You are welcome to stay and share the scones, Mr. Withering," said his client. "I believe the Vicar is bringing his latest canto and intends to read it to me."

"God save us. I shall make my escape while I can. It is not that I disrelish seeing Samuel, but only that once a week is sufficient."

"As if you attended divine services once a week!" said her ladyship in derision. "Once in a season is far closer to the mark."

The lawyer dropped his eyes sheepishly. "Well, you know, he and I have never agreed. Not since we were lads. Now that we are grown and he has come back to Penwith in the guise of this great spiritual transformation, I confess I find it hard to bear that my old school rival should now be my spiritual guardian."

"Not to mention that it is chafing to have a psychopomp who is an acknowledged sportsman, eh?" She pressed upon his vanity without a qualm. "They say he is a great whip. I imagine he makes you eat dust?"

This was a telling shot, for it was as much the Vicar's reputation as a demon-driver as his abstruse sermonising that distanced him from his parishioners, but Withering chose to be fair about it.

"Since we were mere boys and scuffled over your favours, he has made me 'eat dust', as you put it, one way or another."

"And twenty-five years later you are still contending? What a sly flatterer you are, Jonathan Withering. And a man of the law, too!"

He spread his hands as he rose from the chair. "Like the dial in the garden, your ladyship, I tell only the sunny hours."

At that moment a clatter in the drive riveted their attention. "Good lord," Withering murmured, "I am too late." He collected his hat and stick, peered apprehensively through the window, and shuddered as, swaying from side to side, the

Vicar's high-perch curricle flew toward them. Falsworth was at the reins, as usual, the groom behind. That they had travelled a smart distance was evident, for the horses were in a rare state, heavily lathered and all but winded, the foam blowing in long streams away from their mouths.

"Whip, you say? No true whip'ld handle his team like that," Withering muttered and would have had more to say on the subject, but Falsworth curbed abruptly and drew to a tight halt, threw the reins to the groom who had already leapt to the gravel, and bounded towards the house. Withering hurried into the hall so as not to be trapped into prolonged social intercourse, but, just as he reached the door, the heavy knocker banged on the outside of it. Assuming a stolid expression, the lawyer opened the door and surveyed the interloper in a tolerable imitation of Branston.

"Whom, sir, shall I say is calling?"

"Tell her ladyship that . . . eh? Devil take you, Withering, what are you playing at?" The very reverend nostrils flared as if their owner scented something not to his liking. Brimstone, perhaps. "I haven't seen you at service, by the way."

"Have you missed me, Pastor?" Withering chaffed. "I'll be bound you sang a hoseanna when I didn't appear."

Falsworth seemed to take this in good stead. "Not so at all, though I promise I will raise up a *public* prayer for your soul's salvation if you do not make it your business to be there soon."

They clapped each other gingerly about the shoulders while edging past each other in the doorway; Withering out, Falsworth in.

"Good-bye, Jonathan," called her ladyship from the window and the lawyer tapped his hat smartly as he headed toward the stable in search of his roan.

"What a good chap," pronounced the reverend. "I wonder that you never considered an alliance with him, your ladyship, since you would have none of me? He is a Croesus, they say. Very generous to the church."

The look he received quite withered the question in his throat. Lady Augusta Pentreath was not a person to discuss her marriage prospects, even with her spiritual advisor. If, indeed, he could qualify as such. Lady Augusta sometimes *conferred*, but rarely welcomed unsolicited opinions. Certainly there had been a time when her heart had *been* engaged, but not by Falsworth nor by Young Withering. That was long since and, while it would be untrue to say she never thought of the gentleman, it was verity that she no longer dreamed of him in an intimate context.

She rang for the scones. "Cook is your devoted slave. I cannot fathom how you do it, since she will scarcely allow me the time of day. If I have the impudence to venture into her domain, I find I am treated as the rankest intruder. Perhaps, when I am gone, you will persuade her to the vicarage?"

"Gone?" The vicar was startled and the word cracked about the room. "What do you mean, madam? Where are you going?"

Carefully, but with no diffidence, she unfolded her plan.

"Pshaw, you can't be serious!"

She had expected this. "Oh, quite serious, I do assure you."

He considered, meditatively sipping the while. "Demmed fine tea, this."

"Try the scones."

=== 2 ===

LADY CHRISTABEL MAWSON, to give her credit, *had* considered the plight of her unfortunate relations quite thoroughly. To say that contemplation of their situation was sweet would be to overstate the case, but her course ran perilously near soul's contamination, although she concealed it from her daughters behind a studied mask of bemused benignity which fooled them not a bit.

They sat in the conservatory of Fogg's Hall savouring the feast of summer's bounty: Hermione sketching still another flower study and Elizabeth greedily popping sugar-dipped berries into her tiny mouth.

"I must say," remarked the mother casually, "that dear Cousin Augusta has always seemed marked for the worst luck in the family, but how *well* she has survived it, eh?"

"What do you mean, Mamá?" asked Hermione, accenting the title in the fashionable Gallic manner.

"Wel-l-l . . ." considering, almost savouring ". . . to begin with she had almost no suitable marriage offers . . . and then that sudden wedding trip to the continent, which everyone said was so modern, but which we all thought *highly* suspicious . . ." She paused with studied delicacy. "I am not at all sure I should be saying this to you." But the girls did not follow her lead and she was forced to proceed without being begged. "Then, you know, to have been virtual mistress of Pentreath for so many years only to lose it. (They say it was poor Radclyffe who ruined them, but *I* say it is the woman who manages the purse.) And what has she left? That pokey little house in St. Buryan and no money to speak of. It does make one's heart cry. Pentreath was *such* a handsome house!"

"Hadn't you ever hopes of marrying Cousin Radclyffe, Mamá?" asked Elizabeth wickedly. "You would have been a countess."

"Oh, I believe there *was* some talk of it between our families, you know, but nothing came of it. I am sure I was just as happy to marry your father, even though he was only a younger son. Fogg's Hall offered such a wealth of opportunity for improvement, and look how well everything turned out."

"Just think, Hermione," Elizabeth giggled between berries, "if Mamá had married Cousin Radclyffe you would be Lavinia and I should be the beautiful Barbara. What fun that would be!"

"I shouldn't mind," said her sister. "I should be a countess in my own right, and I believe Lavinia has a great love of nature."

"Which she indulges by clumping about out of doors in the wet," observed Lady Christabel tartly. "So much nicer here in the conservatory where you do *your* appreciating, isn't it?"

Delicately she arranged the folds of her sprig muslin into a more pleasing fashion, then sat up very straight, putting her shoulders back as if commenting upon her own invulnerable situation. "I am sure I don't know what they shall do now. Marry farmers, I daresay, and make themselves miserable. What a comedown for an earl's offspring. At least one must say for Augusta that when she couldn't get what she set her heart on, she did very well at second best."

"Oh, Mamá, how funny you are."

Her Ladyship favoured her youngest with a hard stare. "And, pray, Elizabeth, what do you mean by that? I am not sure, but I do believe that even at that dreadfully expensive school you attend they cannot teach you to ridicule your mother *quite* so flagrantly. It is not in the best taste, even though I know you consider yourself very adult and your mother hopelessly old-fashioned."

"Oh, Mamá," Hermione groaned.

"Oh, Mamá! Oh, Mamá! As usual the two of you echo each

other admirably, but . . . as usual . . . I am left waiting for an explanation."

"Well, Mama dear," said Elizabeth in a straightforward English way, "what I mean is that I think it awfully rum of you to sit commiserating about a cousin you have never made bones about holding in abhorrence."

"I am sure I never said that to you or anyone else. It is true that Augusta and I are of quite different tempers, but you go too far.

"And," she added "I wish you to avoid using that dreadful language your brothers bring in. 'Rum' may be well enough for a Corinthian, but not for a well-brought-up young girl."

Did Eliza say 'stuff' under her breath?

"You have always implied it, Mama," Hermione averred as she outlined the saucer-shaped cenothera. "On many occasions when Elizabeth and I would have loved to entertain Barbara and Lavinia here you have always scotched the notion one way or another."

"Or when we were to have visited Pentreath," Elizabeth added. "Not to mention the boys."

Lady Christabel's face had gone quite stiff. "I am sure I did no such thing. Certainly I am not responsible for the way the world turns out. Probably it was never convenient. Those girls know as well as you that my health is subject to vagaries. Would you be so heartless as to condemn your mother to her chamber so that you might race giggling up and down the stairs with cousins whom you hardly know? I had thought better of you." Her expression belied her words, giving rather the impression that this was exactly what she would expect of such ungrateful offspring. She managed to be so adroitly pained that the young ladies in other times would have been quite contrite. "And I am sure I do not know what you mean about your brothers."

"You don't know that Ralph has nourished a *tendre* for Barbara since she was twelve?"

"Pish! Childish nonsense he has long since outgrown."

"Not Ralph, Mamá," said Hermione, "as you would know if you only cared to do so."

Rather than complain again of being badly treated, Lady Christabel resorted to another of her stock responses. With a delicate irony she murmured, "And I suppose you will now say that Jack loves Lavinia?"

"Even we should not go so far as that to plague you," laughed Eliza. "Poor Jack never thinks of anything but shooting and land conservation. Riding to hounds is his religion, I swear."

"Do not blaspheme."

"I don't, Mama, not in the least. Don't you remember last year when he had a fox brought to him on a Saturday for the Monday hunt, and kept it in a tub over the Sabbath?"

"How is that unusual? Many sportsmen do the same."

"Oh, but do they, when they find the creature has escaped, ride to hounds through the churchyard on a Sunday to bring it back? Jack is dear but so dull, Mama, that I imagine he will never marry and you shall be mistress of Fogg's Hall all your life."

"Heaven forbid!" snapped Lady Christabel. "To contemplate contending with rank ingratitude all my days? Never mind it, I pray you. I look forward to the dower house, where I shall live alone and answer to no one but myself."

Hermione, biting her lip with concentration, carefully coloured her primrose a bright yellow. Elizabeth dipped the last of the berries in sugar. "You would be dead bored in a week, I think, and screaming at your shadow."

Fogg's Hall was neither new nor old, having been built some seventy years before on a plan already out of date. When new, it had been draughty and ill-advised and time had not improved it, though it was held in some affection by its inhabitants. Even Lady Christabel had a stake in this dowdy pile for it was she who had conceived and raised the very conservatory in which they now sat. She had it in her mind, when the girls were settled, to have a new front built more in the fashion. In truth the house suited the family very well, being neither too large for them nor too small, being well enough aspected and having the advantage of being within riding distance of the famous Cheyne Spa, summer haunt of the fashionably unwell. Lady Christabel never allowed herself or her children to be seriously unwell, but it was comfortable to be near such an undoubted center of the *ton*. One could mix or not as the occasion arose. Indeed, Ralph would have been there from season's debut until its end if she would have allowed it, but she was too careful to put him in the way of following Cousin Radclyffe's example. The gaming was held at private houses and thus bypassed the gambling laws, but it was available nonetheless and Ralph was only a foolish boy.

Actually, Ralph's taste was for a rather poetic kind of romance. As well as his cherished *tendre* for his cousin, he was always on the lookout for the emotional opportunity and was forever being disillusioned. Since Barbara had always maintained a warm, friendly demeanor towards him, rather than the sentiment he longed for, he had few hopes in that direction, but one day, he was sure, lightning would strike and his future be revealed in a flash. Until then he must wait and keep hopes high. He was at an age when many things served to distract him, and optimism was always high.

"I say," he called out as he breezed into the conservatory, "I have such news!" He bent to kiss his mother's cheek and to indicate with a congratulatory smile his appreciation of Hermione's evening primrose. "Do you know what they are saying in town? Three guesses and the first two don't count!"

"Beau Carlisle is marrying the Princess Amelia," suggested Elizabeth.

"Be serious, do. The Princess Amelia is only thirteen years."

"The Princess Sophia, then," countered Hermione, "she must be a bit longer in the tooth, by now."

"Mother dear, make them stop. This is exciting news!"

At a gesture from their mother the girls somewhat subsided and Ralph let his squib fly. "What do you think, the duke is looking for property in the area!"

"Which duke, Ralph dear?" asked Mama.

"Why, Towans, of course." As if there were no other.

The expression on his parent's face was something to behold. "The Duke of Towans is looking for property in this neighbourhood? How very interesting."

"But doesn't he have a great estate in Rutland?" Eliza queried.

The transfiguration of Lady Christabel did not diminish. "Yes . . . yes, he has an estate near Oakham," she answered in a contemplative voice, "but I believe he spends very little time there. He is a great traveller, I am told."

"And is he very rich?" greedy Eliza enquired.

"And is he handsome?" asked Hermione. "I suppose he must be very old?"

"Very rich *and* very handsome," answered their mother, "and not so old as all that. Only slightly my senior, a very good age for a man. He owns mines in Cornwall, sheep in Yorkshire, as well as a manufactory in the north. Lord knows what all else by this time. Half the kingdom, I should think. He always had an overly acquisitive streak, unlooked for in one of his rank. I daresay he has agricultural interests hereabouts."

"Perhaps he means to take the waters," suggested Ralph. "I must say I am rather off them myself. The stench is abominable."

"And the fees beyond comprehension," said her ladyship. "I allow that I am much taken by the notion of the Duke of Towans becoming a neighbour. It will be much as in the old days."

The excitement which pervaded the conservatory was almost palpable. "You *knew* the duke in the old days, Mamá?"

Lady Christabel smiled enigmatically, but the look in her eyes was revelatory. She touched her hand to her hair. How happy she was that she was the sort of woman who kept her looks. Certainly it was worth the effort. Dear Jeremy, rest his soul, had never looked at her twice after the first year, but that was his way. Still, she remained a handsome woman; her glass told her that. Pity it was wasted. On the other hand, perhaps it was not, after all. Who could tell?

"Wouldn't it be exciting, Mamá, if he married in the neighbourhood and we had a real duke for a neighbour forever? Think of the *ton* it would give the district." She held up her flower portrait. "What do you think, Ralph? I've done it for the sewing room."

"Good place for it. The perfect spot." Hermione flushed with pleasure at the implied compliment, despite the fact that she had never in her life known Ralph to enter the sewing room. He was such a dear. And so handsome for a brother. She loved the way his dark hair fell so naturally into curls across his brow, accentuating its width and nobility. True, his chin was just a trifle feminine, but his fine eyes and sturdy physique outweighed that trifle a hundred times. What a pity it was that he could *not* marry Cousin Barbara; what a handsome couple they would make and what fine children they would have. She hoped she *would* become an aunt one day and that her little nephews and nieces would be worthy of her regard. Nothing could be worse than to have them turn out badly; worse, in a way, than if one married (which she never intended to do) and one's *own* offspring were less than perfect, for one could not even take steps to correct their faults. But what was Mamá saying?

"And you haven't paid a speck of attention to a word I've said, Hermione, have you?"

Contritely, "No, Mamá. I am afraid I was daydreaming again."

Lady Christabel preened her long, handsome neck. "I was saying that we must go to the dressmaker soon. You have such an eye for fabric. I am sure it is your artistic temperament. I think we must all have something new for the season."

"My silk has quite gone off, Mamá. It has faded terribly," Elizabeth complained.

"And all my summer frocks have become much too tight in the bodice since last year," Hermione added. "I hope you will allow us something really fashionable, Mamá."

Their mother hurriedly began to temporise. "Not too fashionable, girls. Remember you have not had your comeout. The outlay for that next year will be horrendous. I had in mind a few muslins and a ribbon or two."

"You'll never guess whom I saw on the street," Ralph interposed.

"But if the duke *should* become a neighbour, Mamá?"

"I could not hold my head up in a faded silk!"

"It was Branston."

Lady Christabel's head swivelled as she gave Ralph her full attention. "You saw *whom*?"

"Branston," he replied negligently. "You remember. The butler from Pentreath."

"You must be mistaken."

"Not at all, Mother. I stopped him to ask after Lady Augusta."

"Indeed?" frostily. "And what did he say?"

"Well, nothing, actually, because Aunt came out of a shop just then."

"Oh, were the girls with her?" cried Hermione. "When shall we see them?"

"She was with another lady, so I didn't like to intrude, but I gather they are coming to Cheyne for the summer."

The young ladies were quite beside themselves with excitement, but Lady Christabel remained self-contained. "And how did she look? Poor soul, I'm sure her sufferings must have taken their toll."

"Not at all. She looked wonderful for a lady of her age."

Her ladyship's nostrils flared ever-so-slightly. "It is no *great* age, is it? I am happy she has kept her spirits up, but, after all, it is the girls who have lost their fortunes. Augusta has money of her own."

"I certainly meant no disrespect, Mother," Ralph interposed quickly. "I know that you and she came out together, but she truly does look quite fine."

"All things considered?" queried his mother acidly.

"Ralph, if you go on you will quite put your foot in it," advised Eliza. "Mama, you know you are the handsomest woman for miles. I cannot think why you are in such a pet."

"I have been thinking," said Hermione seriously. "Do you think I might have a new shawl? Cashmere would be nice and not too heavy. I believe it is still in the swim, is it not?"

"Coming to Cheyne Spa for the waters?" said Lady Christabel. "How very unlike her. I wonder what she has in mind?"

There had always been a vivid rivalry between the two cousins, which in Lady Christabel's case had not been dimmed by time. The knowledge that Lady Lavinia, since the death of the earl her father, was now a countess in her own right, and money or no, took precedence over Christabel's own daughters was bitter as gall. Even the thought of Augusta's brief marriage to that . . . of all things . . . *poet* could not compensate. That had been years ago and she had quite regained her position by now. She wondered if Augusta knew of the presence of Towans. Could that be why she was visiting Cheyne Spa? A woman never forgets, they say, her first love.

= 3 =

WHEN BEAU CARLISLE heard the news of the duke's imminent arrival he felt physically sick at the pit of his stomach. One could scarcely see that he had paled, though, beneath the elaborate layer of maquillage he had so carefully applied before setting out as he did each afternoon. As the Master of Ceremonies of the famous Cheyne Spa, it was incumbent upon him to appear always at his best, despite the continuing inroads of boredom and advancing years, but this news dismayed him to the extreme point of rushing back to his rooms for stimulant. In the best circles alcoholic beverages were not taken before one had made one's social calls, except as medicine. God knew there was no dispute about that on this occasion. For the first time in many years his quiet and secure round of life seemed on the brink of disaster.

One does not reach that perilous fifth decade of one's life without the embarrassing memory of imprudences, and Beau Carlisle was unexceptionable in this regard. In his single-minded effort to rise above his origins there had been more than one moment of what he called to himself 'great unwisdoms'. As regarded the duke, he could only pray that enough years had passed that His Grace would no longer recognise him. The memory, the humiliation of the whipping were with him yet, unfading scars upon his spirit. He had no fear of his name identifying him for he had changed it more than once in the course of his life. Sometimes, sentimentally, he regretted this severing of the links with his past, but it always had seemed imperative. All in all, now, he stood as good a chance as not. How likely was the duke to recognise in the plump, primped, and painted faintly hieratic figure of the ceremonial doyen a shadow from the past? Little chance, little chance of it. Still, one might be justified in fortifying oneself with just a touch more of the medicinal brandy.

He took leave of his chambers once again and went into the mid-afternoon sunlight, moving in a stately fashion and modifying his progress to smile and bow at the silly creatures who thronged here to sip of that revolting liquid which issued from the springs. One taste had been enough for Carlisle and when he observed the diseased condition of many who immersed themselves in the *lustrum*, nothing could have induced him to follow their example. He was quite well, thank you, and had no desire to become otherwise. Let those who would tempt Providence. For his own part he was content, after his duties in the Assembly were done, to repair to the Lower Rooms and fleece them of whatever monies he could extract. The spa, indeed, was as well known for its private games of chance as for its waters. Either, Carlisle reflected, was likely to kill you off eventually.

He smiled syncophantically at the Duchess of Doddington and her omnipresent groom-of-the-chamber. Everyone knew the rogue was supporting his entire family on the largesse of Her Grace. Perhaps that was as it should be, after all. Lord Parnis and his friend the Earl of Russell, the Princess of Pless, the infamous and arrogant Prince Vassili of Russia, and three pretty country girls in the care of their mother were among those who passed and were inspected by Carlisle. Each received the respect due his or her prominence. Truthfully it was Carlisle who was the monarch here. Or so he was to the common mind, a thought which he encouraged, cherishing the esteem, however false, in which he was held. Nonetheless when he met his master he was wise enough to acknowledge him. He went further. To the others in his path he had nodded, or at most touched his brim, but now he raised his hat entirely to the mayor.

"Good afternoon, your honour."

"Afternoon, Carlisle, afternoon. Great news, eh? You've heard, I expect. Best news in a long while. Should be the making of us, am I right, eh? What do you say?"

"Oh, I daresay fine news, sir."

"Eh, what do you mean? What're you saying? How could it be otherwise? Hang it man, are we talking in the same vein? The *dook*, I'm meaning, the *dook* who is coming to live hereabouts. You've heard, I expect, eh? You hear everything."

Beau Carlisle's worst fears were thus confirmed. It was true, then, if Tobias had knowledge of it and he must face into the wind. But with a *good* face. "Ah, yes, I had heard something. The Duke of . . . . Where was it? Tremont? Treginnis? Ah, yes, Upton-Towans, was it not? Well, sir, you know how rumours go, especially in a watering hole."

It was, perhaps, the wrong tack, judging by the darkening of his patron's aura. It seemed to presage storms. Carlisle glanced hastily about to see if anyone had noticed his preoccupation with this gentleman and to head off any diminution of his own outward status. Luckily, no one was near enough to make a difference. To most of the denizens of Cheyne Spa, incurably peripatetic, the likes of Mr. Tobias were faceless collections of respectable and sombre clothes walking upright, which is to say that they did not see him at all. Not to be wondered at, for there was nothing remarkable to see. It was all inside, all in the head, in the acute mind, although an occasional hint sprang into his marble-green eyes. The mayor was the most powerful man in Cheyne Spa bar none, for he was the head of the Corporation, and it was the Corporation which administered everything that mattered: the waters (both above and below ground), the Rotunda, the Assembly, the streets, the houses which were hired out for such smart sums, and even the prosperous lending library, which all the ladies frequented in hope of procuring the latest novel by Mrs. Yonge or Mrs. Fenwicke.

Mayor Tobias did not so much as change expression with Carlisle's dismissal of his news, but a minute flicker of an eyelid enforced his next words. "See here, you'd better hope to blazes the rumours are true. There is no better lure for the gulls than the nobility, and if our Cheyne Spa is good enough for a *dook* to take residence, whether or no he is one with whom the Master of Ceremonies is acquainted, then he is bound to be a draw. I shouldn't have to tell you, sir, that we face mighty competition. Wasn't it bad enough that Bath and Cheltenham drew away our custom without the Swiss and the blasted Austrians putting their fingers into it?" His tone became strained, though his expression changed not a whit. "See here, Carlisle, you'd better cultivate this *dook*, is my advice. He's money in the bank and the Corporation is fond of money . . . mighty fond."

It was to Carlisle's credit that he did not quail in the face of this expressionless tirade, but continued to smile affably as if his co-conversationalist were merely chatting on some social topic. It was this very trait of equanimity which had kept him thus far. "Quite so, sir. I merely counsel against premature rejoicing. His Grace has not, I understand, definitely purchased property nor even taken a private house?"

The glint faded from the verdian eyes. "Well, as to that you may be right enough, but to save your bacon you may hope that it will prove true. You have a feathery spot here, my friend. Better than some you have endured, if I am not mistaken. Pity to compromise it, eh?"

"A great pity," Carlisle agreed fervently. He, himself, might be the ruler of the spa, but Tobias was always there; the power behind the throne. He spied deliverance trotting toward them. "Ah, Countess, shall we have the pleasure of seeing you to-night? The dancing, you know, begins at six. I shall anticipate your presence, madame, with all my heart." When he had finished making his leg Mr. Tobias had moved on. The moment was survived.

Although the Beau arose late in the day, others did not. The efficacy of treatment was said to be closely connected with early diurnal application and, thus, the patient was likely to be wrapped in flannels while a chill was still upon the air and carried by four lusty chairmen to the baths in a little black box just the size of a coffin upended. There a reunion with society was effected on the plea of health. The invalid, in communal relaxation, a floating tray beside her on which reposed her comfit-box, her necessary handkerchief, and a clove-stuffed citrus against the stench, soaked in the naturally hot water. Whatever the baths themselves may have done, the early hours and the exercise which followed the soak accomplished wonders. Later, of course, there was the daily public promenade to the accompaniment of a tolerably good brass band. There the sexes mingled and coffee houses were ready. It was all much more relaxed than in London. As the Beau had said, the balls began at six on Tuesdays and Thursdays, other nights being occupied with theatricals and private parties.

But always there were the gaming tables.

Some said the waters were an excuse, yet, on the other hand, the gamesters rarely stirred themselves before eleven, so the treatment might have failed in any case. One could usually tell the gamblers from the invalids; both were somewhat lacking in colour, but the gamesters often had a pinched look that the others lacked. Perhaps it was worry, perhaps avarice. The gaming laws had not been relaxed, but there was a certain official tolerance now that the old King's eye was not upon them. One could pretend that one was in a mere social gathering and playing for pennies, or one could belong to a club. Brook's, in town, was such a place, but here the play was in the very Lower Rooms; Carlisle's decision. He was certain he would have the Corporation behind him as long as money was being made.

His duties kept him away from the tables in the evenings, of course, but once the theatricals were over and the dancing done nothing hindered him from entering the play. Or leaving it at dawn. Often considerably poorer. Yet on the whole he ruled well. It was due to Carlisle that the spa kept its éclat when others had dimmed. Bath remained, of course, as it always had done; and Cheltenham stood up pretty well to the modern age; but where were the others? Travellers were freed somewhat and went other places in search of spicier adventures. The easing of international rancour was not fine for all.

The lady now approaching the Master of Ceremonies was

certainly not a continuing resident of Cheyne, yet he fancied he knew her face. Good bones there, wide-spaced eyes, and a broad forehead. The silver strands in the auburn hair gave it an attractive shimmer in the afternoon light. To his great surprise the lady smiled at him in a reserved way and called him by name.

"Mr. Carlisle, is it not?"

The Beau made his leg and protested, "But I fear you have the advantage of me, madame." On closer inspection she proved to be quite a handsome piece of goods, well worth his attention.

"I am Lady Augusta Mabyn."

"At your service, madam. Am I correct in believing that you have not been a visitor here for very long?"

She agreed. "Only a day or two, and I shall be staying but a day or two more. That is why this is such a fortunate meeting." She turned to the manservant accompanying her. "I think you may go on with those errands, Branston. I am sure Mr. Carlisle will escort me."

"Delighted, madam." When the servant had gone the Beau ventured to ask, "I anticipate that you have a request to make of me?"

She looked at him sharply as though sizing him up; assessing him, as it were. "You are a good judge of character, sir. I had no idea my intentions were so transparent."

"When you deal with the public, madam. . . ." he shrugged in an affected fashion.

"Yes, I daresay it must be draining to have so many calls upon you. You will be happy to know that I would like to speak to you upon a matter of business. Advantageous business, I envision."

Carlisle's eyes became a good deal more keen. "Advantageous to whom, ma'am?" He appreciated her reply.

"Why, to both of us, sir, but perhaps even more to you than to me."

What she said to him as they strolled along the crowded promenade interested him highly, but surprised him a good deal coming from a lady of certain quality. "Do you understand,

Lady Augusta, that this is a risky business for a woman? You stand to lose a great deal, both in a monetary sense and a social one."

She patted his arm familiarly, as if they were old cronies. "That is why I have come to you, sir. It seems to me that you might, if you chose, alleviate my anxiety on both counts."

"And how could I do that, milady?" Now he was becoming a little wary of her. She was sharp, no doubt of it. That might be all to the good, or it could work in the opposite direction. Well, talk costs nothing. He would make no promises.

"To begin with I think we both know that you are the acknowledged panjandrum of Cheyne. No, do not protest. I mean it in the best sense. You *do* rule here. In the name of the Corporation, perhaps, but it is to you that all social arbitration falls, eh?"

"Perhaps," admitting nothing.

"Thus it follows that your sponsorship would . . ." Her ladyship stopped in mid-sentence and her hand flew to her mouth. She walked on, but her enquiring gaze was turned toward the street. Carlisle's glance followed hers and his heart sank within him. It had come. The moment he had dreaded for years was about to be thrust upon him.

In a high-perch curricle behind a splendid pair of bays rode two gentlemen; one quite young, the other in early middle-age. The youth was handsome enough in a careless, unformed way, but the older of the two was of surpassing distinction. Perfect tailoring enhanced an athletic figure, but it was not in his form that his dignity lay, rather in the severe handsomeness of his face: the strong jaw, the jutting chin, the beak of a nose which dominated his features. Add to this the steel in his hair and a matching steely self-containment that hung about him like an aura. Truly an aristocrat.

The youth made some comment and the gentleman nodded briefly, squandering not a movement, but looking, though, at his companion rather than the promenade. In a moment or two the equipage had passed on along the street and, turning, was hidden from the sight of the two who looked after it.

Lady Augusta was the first to break the spell of silence by opening her parasol (coquelicot in hue and imparting a vastly flattering tone to her complexion) and finishing her sentence as if there had been no interruption of any sort. ". . . your sponsorship would go far in allaying any misgivings in the mind of our spa society."

"I daresay that may be true, madam," Carlisle said, "but how does an advantage fall to me in all this?"

Her smile was both wry and insinuating. "Through money, sir. I anticipate that my scheme might be worth a large amount of money to each of us."

"You are thinking of us as partners?" he asked.

"In a limited way."

The Beau nodded gravely. He held many private doubts about any woman being able to stem the tide of opinion, but, on the other hand, there were indications that his world might soon be set about his ears. It was always well to look ahead. "I will give it my consideration," he promised. The lady favoured him with another restrained smile.

"I thought you might." When she moved away from him, Carlisle saw that her manservant had perhaps been following them all the time as they strolled. Well enough. The lady demonstrated an admirable sense of forethought and caution. She might well prove to be a worthy ally.

4

THE GIRLS WERE not pleased when Lady Augusta disclosed her plan to them a few days later on a visit to their school. "A gambling parlour!" Lavinia cried, so taken aback by her aunt's announcement that she could scarcely believe her ears. "I do not know very much about such things, but surely such places are illegal?"

"Oh, yes, quite illegal," agreed Lady Augusta calmly, "except, if you can believe it, *in a royal palace*. Does that not tell you something of the state of affairs in this country? The Prince Regent is not about to relinquish his own fun, but the morals of the nation must be kept up to standard. The beauty of *my* plan, you see, is that it would not be public at all—merely a few friends stopping by for an evening's diversion. Why, Lavinia, what sort of woman do you take me for?" she asked archly. "Would I flout the law?"

"How would you go about it?" asked Barbara, intrigued despite herself.

"I shall give parties. In places like Cheyne Spa there are always parties of one sort or another."

But Barbara was not content with such an answer and eyed her suspiciously. "What sort of parties, Aunt?" she probed.

"Why, every sort. Ridottos, routs, private concerts, every kind of entertainment that is fashionable. But always a gambling room for those who are neither social nor cultural."

"It is bound to make people talk," warned Lavinia practically. "How do you envision dealing with that?"

"The oldest way in the world," she was answered. "By

ensuring that society is on *our* side. In Cheyne Spa, where I likely will settle, society *is* Beau Carlisle. No one else matters in the least. His dictates are followed slavishly. Carlisle is the judge, the critic, the arbiter, and . . ." she allowed her fine-cut lips to curl ". . . he is a very devil for gaming. The sort who will play till dawn and watch the sun come up on his winnings."

"It all seems very amusing to you, Aunt, but for us it could be ruination!" fretted Barbara. "Who would associate with us? I think it is dreadfully unfair to force us into Coventry just for money!"

The young ladies were completing their final year at Pecksniff Academy, an establishment so select that no more than twenty misses were ever in residence. The school was devoted absolutely to preparing its charges for a dazzling social future. Only last year one of the 'old girls' had married a viscount and another was betrothed to the son of an earl. The fact that Lavinia was a countess in her own right made the sisters' future seem very bright indeed, if all went well. But gambling hardly seemed the way to ensure it.

"For myself," said Lavinia, "I have no great urge to marry. I should be happy to follow in your shoes, Aunt, and live a single life forever."

"You forget that I *was* married," said Lady Augusta. "Briefly but honestly."

"It is all very well to be unconventional," Barbara said, "if one has the money for it. With money one can snap one's fingers at the world.

"Though I shall certainly marry," she added. "There is no question of that."

"Perhaps that is the solution, then," said the aunt. "Barbara shall marry and Lavvy will live quietly with me." But Lavinia would have none of it when it was presented that way.

"I am sure I have as good a right to marry as Barbara," she protested, "whether I choose to do so or not. I must think of the title, after all. It will die out if I do not have an heir."

"You shall both certainly marry," said Lady Augusta, her purpose served.

"And we *must* have a comeout," said Barbara. "I think you forget who we are."

"Not heiresses, anyway," sighed Lavinia. "Perhaps Aunt's is the best way."

"No, not heiresses," said Barbara bitterly. "It is well enough for you; you always seem to find things to do. If nothing else you read a book or go for one of your long walks on the moor, but I should go mad with that kind of life. I don't know if I could live without balls and parties." She looked about her at the walls of the school parlour. "After all, we cannot live *this* sort of life forever. I mean to say, Aunt, that if we were not intended for the great world, there was no point in *finishing* us. We might liefer have been *educated*. Lavinia would have preferred that, I know."

"Would you, Lavvy?" asked her ladyship interestedly. "What would you have done with it?"

"I have no notion, Auntie, and neither does Barbara. She is talking through the air again. If I were to be a governess, perhaps, or if I had a passion for training girls in a school like this. Even here, you know, we are mostly taught by masters who come in. The mistresses seem to know very little."

"Enough for me," said Barbara.

"I daresay," her sister rejoined drily. Then she put a shrewd question to Lady Augusta. "What is *our* position to be in Cheyne, I wonder? Are we to be table-girls or merely the lures to draw the gamesters? My title should be worth a good deal, I think."

"I am sorry you see this in such a light, my dear. Naturally, I had no notion of your being anywhere on the premises. I think it best that you remain here for the time being."

"Here?" wailed Barbara. "At school? We've been here for an age already! Do you mean to say we are to miss all the diversion of Cheyne Spa while you reign outrageous? I call that grossly unfair, Aunt Augusta."

"I shall not be entering upon my course until spring at the earliest," said her aunt. "You will come to St. Buryan for the holidays if you choose. We shall all miss Pentreath greatly at Christmastime, I fear."

They all fell silent thinking of the great Yule celebrations of the past, the parties and the feasting, the goodwill and the good cheer between master and servant alike. "Well, that's all gone, isn't it?" said Lavvy practically.

"Nothing will ever be the same again," Barbara moaned. "This scheme of Aunt's will ruin us altogether in every way."

"I am doing what I see to be the quickest and least dangerous way to fund *your* season, Barbara. It is a buyer's market when one has no capital. Lavinia, at least, has her title, which always fetches something. Her husband will not benefit directly but her son would, or her daughter, for that matter, just as she has done." Lady Augusta referred to the fact that the earldom of Pentreath passed not through the male line alone, but through *heirs of the body* irrespective of sex.

"If you can arrive at an alternate solution, please, by all means, apprise me of it," said her ladyship with something of a bite to her tone. "I shall be most heartily glad to be shed of the responsibility."

She closed her reticule with a firm snap and placidly looked about for her gloves. The young ladies hardly seemed to notice her chagrin and she did not intend to parade it.

"I only hope Aunt Christabel does not come to hear of all this," Barbara continued. "Lord only knows what she would find to say."

"Do not blaspheme, dearest," said her aunt pleasantly. "It isn't at all your style."

"What is, then, I should like to know?" Barbara was determined to be in a pout and not clever enough to see that it availed her nothing.

"I should hope," said the Countess Lavinia, "that it might be to see that Aunt Augusta has been shown most caring about our futures when she needn't have done at all. Why not go and wash your face with cold water, Barbara dear? You are quite flushed. It may improve your temper as well."

When her sister had gone Lavinia laid her hand upon that of her aunt. "Do not take her to heart, pray. She is frightened, I think. We always thought we should have all the good things of the world forever."

"I surmise that such a phrase means quite different things to you and to Barbara," said Lady Augusta with a sigh. "Shall you mind terribly when I put my plan into action?"

The Countess Lavinia actually giggled. "Lud, no. I am looking forward to being quite wicked. I hope you will not short-change me of it in the name of morality, Aunt. As you say, we must each make our own way in this world. But why wait until spring?"

As Branston was driving her ladyship back toward Cheyne Spa, Augusta had ample leisure to contemplate her situation. It seemed to her that all of her life had been lived on the rim of safety, both through her own doing and through the frivolous character of her brother. She fervently hoped for better with Lavinia and Barbara; each had something to barter, after all. Lavinia had her title, and Barbara her truly ravishing beauty. She *must* help them to safe havens.

Nothing in her past had prepared Lady Augusta for the vicissitudes of life in which she had found herself since the death of her brother. First it had been the pressing problems of estate management and maintaining a style commensurable with Lavinia's new rank and educating the girl to her responsibilities. There had never been any question but that Radclyffe would live, as his forbears had done, to a ripe old age and the question of Lavvy's future settled properly by her parent. The task was taken over by her aunt, not unwillingly, but *unsurely.* The loss of the manor house exacerbated the situation vastly. Not that the estate was entirely dependent upon the house. It still functioned, perhaps better without the drain placed upon it by the manor, but the principles which the now Countess Lavinia must learn to apply had not yet been tutored. It was not that Augusta had never been in straitened circumstances. As a young widow in a foreign country she had lived by her wits for a substantial period, but that was for *herself*; the chances she took were with her own life, not another's. An annoying thing was that Lavinia seemed quite content to *let* her aunt involve herself, without showing any inclination towards managing her own life. Lady Augusta had no yearning for power, she had no desire to be proctor a moment longer than necessary. But she *would* continue as long as needed.

The carriage seemed to have acquired an annoying sway as they drew farther away from the village. Branston, so efficient about the house, knew little more than she did.

"I expect it is something to do with the undercarriage, madam," he said not very helpfully. "I shall look out for a smithy along the way. I daresay the smith will be able to put it right."

"Perhaps, next time we drive out, we should hire both carriage and driver?" Lady Augusta suggested diffidently. She had no desire to hurt his feelings, but even Branston could not be expected to be all things to all men.

The line of his back grew pronouncedly straighter. "I daresay, madam, if that is what you wish."

"I would still need your attendance, of course. I could not travel with a strange driver."

"Naturally, madam."

The interchange languished. Branston, laconic at best, had the road to attend and Lady Augusta had her thoughts. How strange it had been to recognise Towans in Cheyne Spa, for she was sure it was he, even though she had not seen him for twenty years. Those faces with prominent cheekbones never seem to change much, she mused. It was not that she had not thought of him in all that time. How could one forget the man who all but jilted you when you were an impressionable and insecure young woman? But she had forgiven him long since. Undoubtedly it had been as a direct result of his sudden elopement with the Chambers girl that she had fallen into the arms of Paul Mabyn, and she had never been sorry. Logically, if he had lived, Paul's ways might have driven her to distraction—that endless, tuneless whistle, for example, had already begun to wear—but she had loved him, there was no question of that. Towans was no lost romance seen through eyes dimmed by nostalgia, but it might be amusing to meet him again. Had he remarried, she wondered, after the death of his wife? God knew he was still quite eligible.

And the girls needed husbands.

And who had been the young man with him? Her quick look had pronounced him presentable, but was he merely a servant? Probably not, for their manner had seemed intimate. Was he, then, a mere companion or—it must be considered—a relation unacknowledged in polite society? The duke would not be the first who took his bastard as, say, his secretary.

But why on earth was her mind running along these lines? It might be the most innocent relationship in the world, after all. The lad might be the son of a friend, or a nephew unknown to her.

He might even be eligible.

5

AT ABOUT THE time Branston had begun driving his mistress back toward Cheyne Spa to further her plans, His Grace the Duke of Towans was attempting, with as little success as usual, to impart a few grains of wisdom to his young friend Gerald.

"It never does, my boyo, to exhibit a heavy hand. Tends to worry the mouths of horses and overweights one's position in society."

"Are you suggesting, sir," Gerald queried somewhat truculently, "that I should have allowed that cony-catcher to continue on the path he had taken?"

"There are a great many fools in this world, I am sorry to say. If you find it necessary to give tuition to all of them you will find yourself a very busy young man. Lice like Filer are not worth the attention."

"But he was cheating!"

"Only by an acceptable amount. It is called clever card playing."

"I call it dishonesty!" Gerald averred stoutly and His Grace chuckled. The boy had spirit.

"You'll have plenty of time to call him on it. I wager he's only begun. Why not wait until his behaviour is in no way redeemable? Do you know what they say of him in London? It was making all the rounds just before he was shut out of Almack's. Rather clever, I think. That he is a gentleman of four 'ins'."

Gerald was puzzled, even after considering for a moment or two. "I don't follow that at all, I'm afraid."

"Nor did I until it was elucidated," agreed the duke. "It seems that a gentleman of four 'ins' is this: *in* debt, *in*-dicted, and *in* danger of being hanged *in* chains!"

Gerald laughed dutifully, but he was not to be mollified. "I still say that he is a cheat and a blackguard, and that no gentleman should sit at table with him . . . for cards or anything else. I certainly shall not."

"See that you don't. For one thing I doubt you can afford it."

The young man pulled out his pockets ruefully. "You see my fortune," he said. "What I shall do in future I cannot imagine."

"What all personable young wastrels do, I daresay," said His Grace. "You'll find yourself a pretty little wife with a pretty little dowry and settle down to raise up pretty little children who do not follow in their father's footsteps."

Gerald pulled a face and settled into a chair with the newest gazette as the duke looked fondly at him.

Although he had no real responsibility for the youth, Towans had more or less taken him under his wing since the death of the lad's parents and he had never been sorry for it. Gerald, he said, kept him young, or at least within speaking distance of youth. As for the young man, he had never known the duke as anything but *uncle*, his father's best friend; never thought of him as superior in rank, but only as a friend and confidant naturally superior in all those matters which pertain to a young buck's growth, both physical and moral: that is in dress, gambling, and horsemanship. Although he had a tiny competence from his father, his unofficial function was as a sort of secretary to his grace and in such capacity he performed his duties well. He also, because of his youthful exuberance, provided a good deal of unwitting amusement. In short they were a felicitous pair of wanderers, for the time well suited to one another.

Wandering, in fact, was by way of being their way of life. The duke had been married once upon a time, but that had come to an unfortunate conclusion and, besides the lady was dead. Although he was endowed from birth with a good many noble acres in Rutlandshire, he found the place gloomy and never could bring himself to think of it as home. He never felt himself to have one at all, but, instead, had for many years drifted from place to place, sometimes alone, sometimes in company such as Gerald's. In a vague sort of way he expected sometime to find the place where he belonged, expected to recognise his home by the feel rather than the look of it. Of late he had even begun desultorily looking at tracts of land, wanting to buy and settle but never finding quite the spot. He had even looked in the neighbourhood of Cheyne Spa though he doubted it would ever be here that he settled. Still, who could tell?

Gerald threw down his gazette with a snort. "This thing is worse than the London papers, nothing but nonsense. I expect they'll broadcast next the news that *you* have arrived and I shall be besieged with pleas for an introduction to you. Cannot we go out a bit before that happens?"

"You might meet that heiress you hanker after through being besieged, you know."

"It has been my experience that those who want to meet *you* have precious little time for *me*. Women are far more careful about their fortunes, you know, than men. If they ain't clever they have guardians who are.

"Not that I mind," he added. "I ain't so sure I'd care to be bought."

"And has anyone yet offered for you?" the duke asked with a smile.

"Not that I have noticed. I imagine they have been too busy trying to get past me to you, sir. You're considered quite a catch, I understand."

"So they say," replied the older man without much interest. He had been so assiduously pursued for so long a time that the subject was quite devoid of either charm or interest. When it came to himself and matrimony he could not even rise to his companion's banter, though he was pleased enough when Gerald sprang from the chair with a welcome question.

"Care to ride, sir?"

"I might. Where did you have in mind? Not just about the town, I hope. We have about exhausted the scenic possibilities of gouty gentlemen limping after ladies."

"We might explore outside the town a bit, don't you think? They say there is a famous cavern lurking hereabouts somewhere."

"For the entrance to which they charge a smart fee, I'll be bound. I think I have seen every cavern going and after while they all begin to look the same, whether they are in the Mendips or the vicinity of the Matterhorn. Perhaps geology ain't worth the tariff for the likes of me, eh?"

Although his grace was the most generous of men, as Gerald knew well, the youth could not resist the chance to be respectfully scornful, an impulse which came with the ease of long acquaintance.

"If you don't mind my saying so, Uncle, what difference does the tariff make? You've certainly got it."

His grace cuffed him lightly and called him a cub. "I'll tell you something, that is *why* I've got it. I never pay a penny for a diversion that doesn't divert."

"But you gamble, sir."

"Quite right, my lad, and with notorious sharps sometimes. I expect you consider that I'm throwing my money away, but I don't mind it as long as they hold my interest. I'd a demmed sight rather be fleeced than bored."

They had by now come out to the street, waiting for the horses to be brought round, and Gerald discreetly indicated two people across the way who were in deep conversation. "Speaking of notorious sharps, Uncle, there is your 'gentleman-of-four-ins'."

"Ah, Filer, yes. Who is the youngster he's giving such a dressing? My word, the boy looks quite pea-green."

"I've seen him about," Gerald said. "Name of Mawson, I believe. I expect he's in deeper than he can swim, poor devil. I saw him at the table with Filer last night."

As they rode towards the edge of town the young man's name returned to the duke's mind and he began to muse out loud in a way that was half addressed to Gerald and half to his own self. "Mawson. I think it was a Mawson who married Lady Christabel. By Jove, I swear it was. And from this part of the world, too, I'll be bound. I wonder if the pup can belong to her? What a coincidence that would prove . . . after all these years. See if you can't find out the chap's Christian name, Gerald, and what his antecedents might be."

"Right, Uncle. It shouldn't be too difficult. People at Cheyne Spa seem willing to talk about almost anything or anyone. It must be for lack of better occupation."

"When you are soaking in the minerals," said the duke, "I imagine your mind will turn to any diversion."

To the north of the spa a long line of low hills guarded the horizon and it was in that direction that they turned their mounts. The day was fine and they were comfortable enough with each other that conversation was pleasant but not imperative. For the most part a companionable silence prevailed. When, a few miles from Cheyne, a village appeared upon the path ahead his grace suggested they stop for ale and cheese, then consider turning back toward the spa, since they had no precise destination.

But at the smithy a singular sight caught their eyes. Seated upon a rock at the side of the road was a lady of mature though not yet middle years. She was elegant in a perigord ribbed-silk and was playing at cup-and-ball with a dirty-faced village child. And enjoying herself greatly, if her laughter was to be believed. The child, too, was merry with the game, perhaps because she was winning.

As the men rode up, the child bobbed and retreated while the lady smiled at the two of them in a cordial way, and said, "Good afternoon, your grace. You have chosen a lovely day for a ride. I perceive, too, that your seat has improved greatly since last we met."

The duke doffed his hat. "I am afraid you have the advantage of me, madam." Then he peered at her more closely, scowling a little. "Good Lord, Augusta?" He seemed astonished.

"So you remember me, your grace?"

"Egad, it hasn't been all that long. I was thinking of your cousin, Lady Christabel, not an hour past. It seems like only yesterday that we were all youngsters together."

The lady rose from the stone and smoothed her skirt. "Really? Twenty years is a long time to me, thank you. You must measure time in aeons. Is that a perk of the upper regions or merely the birthright of the Towans?"

The duke's grin had taken on an engaging quality that Gerald had not often seen and he began to pay particular attention to the meeting of these two people. The lady was decidely handsome and of obvious quality. What was also obvious was the light that sprang into the duke's eyes as they talked. "I have it on good authority," his grace was now protesting, "that the line of Towans harks back to the mists of antiquity, madam. I'll thank you not to call it into question."

The lady nodded. "So far into antiquity, they say, that you acknowledge only the Trinity your betters. I would have thought, though, that wandering about in the mists might be very dangerous, especially in fen country where one might so easily fall into bogs."

After a startled moment Gerald decided that the lady knew exactly what she was saying and he hooted at the ribaldry, drawing a cold stare from his mentor. The youth was not sure how seriously he had breached propriety in the duke's eyes, but, after all, the lady had begun it. She smiled to show he was forgiven, at least by her.

"And this braying jackanapes," said his grace, "is my young . . . well, *ward* is as good a description as any, I suppose, though I'll be demmed if I take any real responsibility for his behaviour.

"Gerald," he said, "get down and make your leg to the Lady Augusta Mabyn of Pentreath Manor." The youth obeyed gracefully.

"Gerald Wetherbridge, at your service, madam."

"I would be a fool not to take advantage of such a pretty proposal," said her ladyship. "You might just see what it is takes so long with my carriage at the smithy. My man seems to have been gone an unconscionable time."

"Your carriage is in difficulty?" the duke asked.

"Not mine, only hired. This is what comes of using a hack-chaise."

"My pleasure, madam," Gerald said and was off at a bound. Her ladyship looked after him, then up at the duke.

"Really your ward, Towans, or something more close of connexion?"

The duke dismounted and stood beside her, holding the reins of the two horses lightly in one hand. "If you mean that he is my by-blow, the answer is a definite no. He is merely the son of a friend."

"Wetherbridge? It is not a family I know."

The duke shrugged. "His hat covers his family, I'm afraid. He is quite alone in the world."

"What, such a handsome sprat and no connexions?"

"None whatsoever. Except that he is my friend."

The lady hid a smile to avoid revealing her thoughts. "Hardly a recommendation of which to be ashamed, Your Grace."

"I wish that you would think of me not as a duke, but as a man and your friend. Cannot you call me Richmond, as you did in the old days?"

"I hardly think that would be proper. The old days have long since passed away, even though it does not seem so to you."

He took this well enough and changed the topic by asking her destination.

"Oh, to Cheyne Spa. It is the great watering-hole of this part of the world and easier than a trip abroad."

He seemed amused. "Then you are taking the waters for your health?"

"Lud, no," she answered, fluttering her handkerchief in the manner of a fan. "I had as lief be ill as cured by such a draught. It happens that I have business there concerning the estate of the girls." The handkerchief waved again. "It is difficult being a woman and alone."

"I am sure that is true," he answered her, "but I think we know that this is not the best of all possible worlds."

"Sadly," she said.

"Sadly," he agreed. "But these 'girls' as you speak of them. They are your daughters?"

She looked quite shocked. "My daughters? Good heavens,

how old do you take me for? Barbara is seventeen and Lavvy nearly nineteen. I should have started producing at a very early age." She considered. "Actually, I suppose Barbara *could* be mine . . . and, oh dear, I suppose Lavinia as well." She sat up very straight and looked proper. "But they are not."

Suddenly she found herself pouring out the whole story to this newly found friend from the past; Radclyffe's weakness for the tables, the mismanagement of the estate, and finally the loss of magnificent Pentreath Hall.

"But this oldest gel . . . Lavinia, is it? . . . she inherits?"

"If you can call it that," said Lady Augusta. "Since Radclyffe sold off everything that was not entailed, she has precious little but the title."

The duke grew interested. "What title is that? Do you mean to say it passes through the female line?" When she agreed he said, "But you have something of great value right there. A title *always* fetches something extraordinary. Money in the bank, my dear."

Augusta was doubtful. "Her husband would not benefit."

"But her *child* would benefit," said the duke with the air of teaching a backward student. "The heirs of her body would be the heirs of his as well, as I have reason to know."

For despite their joking the ducal crest of the Towans was of relatively recent origin and the lineage sprang from a disputed side of the bed. Far from being of an ancient line, the first Duke of Towans had the honour of ascribing his paternity to no less a personage than Charles II, that merry monarch who had the foresight to create peerages of one kind or another for most of his acknowledged offspring. That the name enshrined in the title signifies a duchy of shifting sand perhaps indicates the transitory nature of royal relationships, but when Tryphena Trenarry came to court in 1668 as a companion to the fading Countess of Castelmaine she quickly caught the monarch's eye. Shortly her charm and west country complexion had not only eclipsed her sponsor but given her the ascendant. The first Duke of Towans was the result and the present duke a true Stuart, affectionate, generous, and a law only unto himself.

"You say the one's a countess and the other a beauty? Egad, Augusta, bring 'em to Cheyne Spa. We'll have 'em married well within a week!"

= 6 =

IN THE FEW days since she had heard of Towans' presence in the neighbourhood, Christabel had had little time to absorb the idea of his settling in the area. In an uncanny way it felt as if time had run full circle from when they were young people together. The difference was that she had two marriage-aged daughters and he was still eligible. Curious. And interesting.

What had become of him after the desertion of that chit he married? It had been all those years since she had seen him, yet how vividly the memory came back of that last, brilliant Yuletide party at Pentreath. Of course he had only been the young marquess then. The wretched old man, his father, had still been alive and taking every advantage of his age and position.

There had always been a tacit understanding between her family and their cousins, the Pentreaths. That holiday gathering was to have set the seal of approval upon the match between herself and Radclyffe.

Until the old devil had spoiled it!

She remembered acutely how he had followed her into the bookroom on that long-ago afternoon and attempted liberties she would never have allowed her betrothed.

And the look on Radclyffe's face when he came into the room unexpectedly!

Radclyffe had been a poor thing, really, and showed it. No formal offering had yet been made, so there was no question of a jilting nor any sort of scandal. Well, Radclyffe was dead and the old man long since gone to dust and she was the only one who knew that nothing had really transpired that day in the chilly library. Sometimes, in her heart of hearts, she wondered what liberties she *might* have allowed the old duke if it had enabled her to become a duchess.

And now, like a quadrille, all things seemed to be coming round again.

She could hear the girls in the next room, idle and bored. These were dull days when Fogg's Hall by reason of its low-lying situation was enveloped in the mists which sometimes enshrouded its acres for a fortnight at a time. No wonder everyone felt cross and that Hermione showed the tiniest tendency toward whining.

"Do you think that Ralph actually bought the stockings?"

"Lord, sister, how should I know? You asked me the same question not five minutes past, and I still have no answer. You certainly hinted at it strongly enough. It was all but a commission."

Hermione was sighing nervously. "I flatter myself that he did not even hear me when I spoke of them, and I wish that he might not have, for I cannot very well afford to pay for them. All my money seems to have gone in buying white gloves and pink Persian. Everything is so dear. Mercy Loomis says that Irish linen is going for three and sixpence a yard, and too coarse for shifts.

"And I wonder what became of that shopping expedition promised by Mamá? It seems to have evaporated quite away." This was asked in a tone calculated to carry into the next room, but Lady Christabel did not rise to the lure. Her mind was not-so-idly occupied.

Fancy Towans coming back into the picture. She did not believe in destiny, of course, no sensible person did so, nor astrology, yet they did say that every . . . what, twenty eight years? . . . one's life began a new cycle, one had a new opportunity to mend the past or at any rate, they said, reshape the future.

What was Augusta like now? What had she become? They had met once or twice, but the old barriers were always there. The hatreds of youth may transform themselves, but mere enmities remain. She and Augusta had always been poles apart and would be still. Natures never change.

But in "another part of the forest," namely the stables, the line of country was quite different. The girls might lisp and giggle and the mother scheme, but here the talk was of honest, concrete things. Christabel's sons were no dreamers.

"I don't mind saying," admitted Ralph, "that it was a bit sticky for a bit, but I got past him."

"And how did you manage that?" asked his brother, feeling the right foreleg of the filly with expert fingers. Yes, he had been correct, something amiss here. The beast stirred restively, but he crooned softly and she subsided, though shivering, and it was evident that she was in some discomfort. He explored again. There was a definite curb below the hock.

"I outfaced him, rather. He's one of those ratty-faced types, is our Filer, and no bottom at all, from his actions."

Ralph shot him an appraising look. "I shouldn't count on that if I were you. Just hand me that rag there. No, behind you."

"Tell you what," the younger brother burbled on, "I fancy I may have a talent for it."

"What, gambling? That's a fool idea. They all think that."

"Why is it? I look at it being like Hermione's drawing ability, or your knack with horses. God-given, don't y'know? Some have it and some don't have it and can't get it. I daresay it has something to do with the way the brain works, calculation and that. Or perhaps the quickness of the eye."

"There, steady, gel, steady. A poultice'll put that right as rain in no time at all, you'll see." To his brother Jack said, "You'll *have* it in the eye, an' you don't take care. If that chap is a professional then he's no fool. Mind what you're about is what I say."

"You always think the worst." Ralph kicked lazily at the straw bedding, at which the filly rolled her eyes. "Have you ever gambled, Jack?"

Jack, still kneeling, looked up at him in surprise. "What, *me*? No." The genuine openness of his response was a condemnation in itself, or so his sibling read it.

"You needn't be sanctimonious. I daresay you have other vices."

"Do I?" Jack took down the bag of kaolin from the tack shelf and began to mix a bit of it with a generous amount of spit. "I shan't ask *you* to join me in 'em, at any rate. Mine be private vices."

Deftly the china clay poultice was applied and the filly soothed. "See there, m'gel? Not half bad was it, eh? Have a nice rest for a day or two and you'll be dancing with the best of 'em." He patted her on the flank and was rewarded with a soft nicker.

"Lookit," he said to Ralph, "let's just run it down, shall we?"

"Oh, very well," with a resigned sigh, "but I can't think what you expect to accomplish."

"Nobbut making you take a sharp look about you. You're being a gull as I sees it."

"No such thing," Ralph said quickly and with a certain amount of heat.

"Perhaps not. Run it down, though, eh? Where'd you meet this chap?"

Ralph frowned in concentration, trying to visualise the exact scene. "In the lower rooms. I was alone, don't you know, and hanging about watching. When his partner was taken ill Filer asked me if I would be so kind as to take his hand until the chap came back . . . which he didn't . . . and we played and took the rubber."

"Then he stood you a drink, I'll wager."

"How did you know that?"

"And you more or less drifted back into a friendly game between the two of you, Filer dealing."

Astonished. "Were you there? I had no idea. Why didn't you hail me?"

"I wasn't there, but that was what happened, wasn't it?"

"Yes, but I won the first two games. I could have got up from the table and left the chambers."

Jack's laugh was as sardonic as his sunny nature would allow. "Ah, but you didn't. No sport could not give the chap a chance to win his money back."

"Well, no. Only proper, that."

"Certainly. But then he won . . . quite a bit, I imagine. He was better than you had thought."

Ralph wrinkled his nose at that. "Not better, only for the moment a bit luckier. You can't judge by a mere game or two."

"My sentiments exactly. Don't judge yourself that way either. But let me go on . . . gradually he allowed you to play for credit. Right? And then, when you were in steep, what happened?"

"As I told you. I outfaced him and my luck turned. That was a day or two later, but I won it back, all I had lost."

"Don't it strike you at all odd?"

"Not a bit of it. I say, I can't help but wonder why you're being such a nimenog about this. You're not jealous, are you? Because if you are I can tell you right off that I'd give a lot to be able to do the things you can do. I saw you with the filly. You have healing hands, brother. That's a rare gift."

Jack was quite nonplussed. "Naught wrong with her that a bit of rest won't cure. And as for being jealous, I wouldn't be so mean-minded as to put you off something you pleasure in. I only want you to be clever about it and not skinked by a slippery fish."

Ralph chuckled. "Filer won't be taking me in, I can tell you. Between the two of us, I fancy he's a bit under the hatches a good bit of the time. I hope you're not going to pull a long face and talk morals to me about it."

"Just don't get in over your head, Ralph, is all I ask. Remember that you've nothing to fall back on if you hit a squall." As soon as he said it, he was sorry, for the look Ralph shot him bespoke volumes. Quickly Jack dropped his arm about his junior's shoulders.

"That's the official line, you know. Mam would never stand for anything else, she's that worried about the estate. Between us, if you get skint there might be a bit of succor. I promise nothing, mind, but there might be." He squeezed the shoulders as they made their way through the mist toward Fogg's Hall.

Lady Christabel, seeing them through the window, could not but contrast their natures. Pity that Jack could not share more

56

of his younger brother's sunny disposition, but then there was no denying that Jack was like his father, of the earth earthy, and Ralph her own duplicate in temperament. Ralph was such a comfort. She could not believe that it was only in her own eyes he was a *non pariel*.

In Cheyne Spa, too, the inclement weather confined folk to their chambers and worked strange moods upon them. Young Gerald so forgot himself as to say to his patron in stunned amazement: "Promised her *what*, sir? You? A sponsor for two undowried young ladies thrusting themselves upon the world?"

The duke stretched in his chair and lighted a cheroot. "Then I astonish you, my boy? I rather thought I might. Should be an interesting experiment, I forsee. I've never played at being uncle to the feminine sex before. Perhaps it is time I began, don't you think?"

Gerald boxed his own ear clumsily. It was no use. He had *not* misheard. And, in fact, he had no idea what to think. None whatsoever.

7

"AND SO YOU can see that she is being absolutely horrid. I am quite beside myself with confusion and distress," Barbara sighed.

Young Withering, allowed in the parlour of Lady Augusta's house in St. Buryan by virtue of being an old family associate, murmured, "There, there, my lady." He had been soothing clients over and over for too many years not to understand the fine points of a privileged relationship and he played them well. Lady Barbara needed a broad shoulder to lean upon and Witherings had always shone in that capacity. Avuncular though the role might be in this instance, the lawyer had to admit it an attractive opportunity.

The door of the room was open, of course, and presently the redoubtable Branston would be wheeling in the ancient tea-trolley to set the seal of respectability upon the meeting. It was not beyond reason to believe that he was even now hovering only inches beyond the sightlines of the doorway. Listening, too, probably. There could be no question of impropriety, but meanwhile these moments of intimacy between himself and the ravishing Lady Barbara were not going to be disturbed by any action of Withering's own.

Barbara was almost relentlessly beautiful this afternoon, though there were tearstains upon her cheeks and a slight puffiness about her lips, which only rendered them more delectable. The young ladies had come back to St. Buryan the day before. Withering had called upon them only to be sure that everything was in order and had found himself knocked flat out by the blossoming Lady Barbara. It was his good fortune, he now knew, that Lady . . . no, *Countess* Lavinia, he must teach himself to think of her . . . was already outside tramping through the gorse, dogs at her heels and the winds in her hair. He hoped she might discover it a fine day for walking. Long walking and far.

"You have not encouraged her in this, I hope, Mr. Withering?"

"I? Oh my, no. When she told me of it I would not even listen."

"You knew of it, then?" Barbara's look was just short of being an accusation, though what she had expected him to do with the knowledge he was sure he couldn't fathom.

"Oh, yes, I knew. Or knew she was contemplating it."

"Did you try to dissuade her?" Why did the girl sound as if he had committed a crime against society? She seemed to believe he had actively abetted the scheme when he had been quite adamant against it. He tried to recollect exactly. He had been, hadn't he?

"Not my place to dissuade," he reminded her, but Lady Barbara gave him such a look of scorn that he wished he had been just a trifle more forward with Lady Augusta. It wouldn't have been out of place, surely, as an old family friend, to remind her ladyship that it was far easier to fall from social grace than to regain one's position once the dreaded label of *declassé* had been applied. "I shouldn't worry, Lady Barbara. Your aunt is a sensible woman who has, for the most part, lived her life in a sensible way."

As soon as he uttered the phrase, he was sorry, for Barbara all but leaped, as they say, like a duck on a Junebug. "For the *most* part? What does that signify, pray? Is there something more about my aunt that I should take into consideration?"

His old friendship with Lady Augusta quite overrode any infatuation with her niece. Loyalty in lawyers might be rare enough but it must exist at some time. "Lady Barbara," he said stiffly, "so far as I know the life of your aunt has been exemplary. You, of all people, I should think, might have little cause for complaint, since she has been for you a mother almost since birth."

Barbara's explanation was almost a wail. "But we had money, then! Now all we have is position." She leaned forward, touching him lightly. "Mr. Withering, have you ever been poor?"

"Not poor, exactly, though my late father's pleasure was to keep me on a tight rein so far as money was concerned," he confided. Why he did so he could not have said. It was hardly suitable that a gentleman of his years and dignity should be exchanging confidences with a young woman of rank, an earl's daughter, no less.

"Let me tell you, sir, it is not pleasant pinching pennies as we have had to do since father's death. Do not misread my words, I beg you. I have nothing but gratitude to my aunt. However, there are limits, it seems to me, at which one must halt."

"I daresay, Lady Barbara, I daresay," Withering said dreamily. What *was* that perfume the girl was wearing? The scent was intoxicating. An alarming surmise that he might be succumbing to an unsuitable attitude crossed the lawyer's mind, compelling attention and thrusting him back into the world of reality. He drew himself up short. Under no circumstances was it possible to allow his personal inclinations to affect his professional standards. "I think you should bear two things in mind, Lady Barbara. First, that whatever Lady Augusta decides to do will be out of loving concern for you and your sister."

"I admit that, sir, but it would not right a wrong, now would it?"

He lifted an admonishing finger. "Secondly . . . secondly, I was about to say, she has, as yet done nothing to which you can possibly object."

She protested but he was delivered by the creak of the tea-cart as Branston pushed it into the room. "Branston," asked the lawyer, "has her ladyship made any mention of her plans in Cheyne Spa?"

But the question, simple and straightforward as it was, proved to be an error. Branston's face froze into an expression somewhere between disdain and pity, while the Lady Barbara seemed merely embarrassed that the lawyer should have asked such a thing of a servant. Whatever rapport had existed between them was certainly ruptured by Withering's lack of finesse.

The redoubtable Branston did not even reply, merely asked with chilly emphasis, "Will you have milk or lemon, sir?" Young Withering did not press the matter.

Actually, he would have found no advantage in it if he had done so, for just then there was a great tumult of overexcited brachets and baying hounds on the lawn. The long window was thrown open and the young countess, redolent of broken fern and gorse, scratched, dirty, and altogether unaware of any diminution, burst into the room and made for the cakes with a greedy cry.

"How wonderful, Branston. Just the thing!" and seizing a fair handful she broke and flung them to the canines clustered about the entry.

"There you are, my darlings. Isn't that a treat?" She turned back to her sister. "You cannot imagine, Barbara, what loves they were today. Do you know that monument they call the Blind Piper . . . or is it Fiddler . . . in the field there by the Merry Maidens?" Then she noticed the visitor. "Mr. Withering! Just the man! You've lived here forever, what is it called?"

The Countess was so exuberant that he could not take her words amiss, and answered them without regard of their expression . . . still, practically speaking, they were a little disparaging. "I believe, your ladyship, that the stones in the *far* field are called The Piper. It was the very battlefield, I believe, on which our Cornish King Howel was conquered by the English under Aethelstan. The Nine Maidens, they say, danced for joy at the victory and were turned into stone for their lack of proper patriotism." The countess seemed to care not a whit for his antiquarian knowledge and flung herself carelessly upon the sofa.

"Tea, Branston! Hot and plentiful, if you please." She saw that she had emptied the plate. "And more cakes. I think it very mean to have so few."

The butler forbore to mention that cook would not be

gratified that the first offering had been flung to the hounds but took away the dish with a small smile. The Lady Barbara was not so easy on her sister.

"Don't you want to tidy yourself a bit before you join us, Lavvy?"

Lavinia merely shrugged. "Am I too gross for company? I think it is merely the fresh air which bothers you. You should come out with me, Barbara, the sun would do you good."

"And leave me brown as you have become? No, thank you. I like my complexion the way it is." Then, remembering their guest, "What do you think, Mr. Withering?"

The lawyer hedged with words about lily-maids and nut-brown maidens, but was not fool enough to commit himself. Lady Barbara paid no attention, in any case.

"Since you are here, Lavvy, we may as well thresh this dreadful situation with Mr. Withering as monitor. You may have a title to bargain with, but I have nothing but my face and reputation.

"You see," she said to Withering, "I must marry well. I could not bear to be poor."

And Withering's heart, not inexplicably, leapt into his throat, for if it were only money that was needed to make her happy! Now he recalled his conversation with her aunt apropos of setting one's sights too high and found himself hoist with his own petard. There was a sort of wrench at his vital parts and his hands trembled, he hoped not visibly. Could she, would she consider? The sensible, legal part of his mind was already pointing out the folly of his emotions, but, swept away, it meant nothing to him. The possibility of possessing this ravishing young creature was addling him and he knew it and he did not care. Oh, if it were only money that was the criterion, there was no problem at all, for lawyers know, he thought proudly, how to extract the sweet kernel from the hardest nut. No, money was not a problem.

If Lady Barbara noted his confusion she paid it no mind, taking it, perhaps, as her due. It may be that she saw, attended and put it away in her acquisitive little mind for future reference. Of such details are great careers compounded, but she returned to the topic of their conversation.

"Is there, sir, not some way she can be prevented?"

This daunted even her admirer. "Do you mean to say legal action?"

"Why, yes, if necessary. It is my own future I must protect."

He came down with a thump from his rose-tinged cloud and gazed at her goggle-eyed. "Do you mean to say you would bring action against your own aunt?"

The sharpness of his voice penetrated even through her rind of vanity and she quickly threw up defences, retreating into girlish ingenuousness, blushing prettily, and said, wide-eyed, "Is that not the way to do?"

And caught him again so deftly that he hardly felt the net.

"No, my lady, for she is your guardian and to take action such as you propose in the face of her loving care of you would injure you far more than any unwise notion of hers."

He moved unconsciously closer and said, "Let us put our heads together to see if there is not a way out of this pickle."

The Vicar of St. Clarus, riding for once astride rather than careering along the roads on the high perch of his curricle, was thoroughly enjoying the day. It was the weather of heaven, the sky a clear cerulean flecked here and there with fleece, the atmosphere of a temperate softness which made the heart sing. The vicar, as it happened, was a single man, for the most part by choice. Let it not be held against the Reverend Falsworth that he had an eye to the main chance. Advancement within the faith comes slowly and is not entirely meted out upon a spiritual basis. The vicar had always been of the notion that his church's patron, Clarus, was something of a fool. Pursued by a rich woman of the nobility he had taken vows rather than surrender his body to her embrace. The lady, feeling, no doubt, that her passions and her rank should override his monastic covenant and his own wishes, had him pursued and murdered, thereby lifting an obscure gelding to the ranks of martyrdom. Falsworth knew that he himself was not such a fool as that. He remained a single man, albeit one with an eye for the main chance. And it was a fair day, a day for lovers and single men.

Approaching along the narrow road past Lady Augusta's house, he was surprised to see the familiar roan of his lawyer standing patiently in the drive near the main door. Had her ladyship returned, then, from her business in Cheyne Spa? As her spiritual advisor he had spoken out against her schemes, but as a moderately fixed man with a sharp eye, he had been much taken with them. He wished her well. By circumstance he had not seen the girls in a year or two; either they had been away at school or he had been absent from his duties. But he apprehended that they must be a trial for their aunt, raised up in comfort by their father, but now reduced to making their own way in the world. It would be easier for them than others, of course. He believed that Lady Barbara had grown into a beauty and with Lavinia came what remained of the Pentreath acres, plus a coronet. No husband of hers would wear it, more was the pity, but it would be no poor thing to be the father of a count or countess. Curious how these inheritances could run.

Around the corner of the house came a rowdy pack of canines, in their midst a young woman of near-maturity . . . and near handsomeness. He calculated quickly. If this were the countess she must be giving her younger sister a bit of a run in the looks department, for there was a freshness and a wholesome quality about her destined to attract a certain kind of man. Falsworth's mouth turned up in the corners. And demmed if he wasn't one of them. Without hesitation he hailed her.

Lavinia came freely across the grass toward the road, hands held open before her and a pleased look upon her face. She was always happy to see this old friend of her aunt's, the more so since he had never feared to endanger his reputation and zestfully followed the hunt as well as indulging his passion for horseflesh and speed. He looked surprisingly the same. Curious how nothing changed here even after two or three years. How wonderful a circumstance that was.

"Vicar! How good it is to see you! And what a good mount!" She walked about the animal, eyeing it in admiration. Large, wide quarters, a rounded and deep chest that promised plenty of heart room, good, straight legs. "What a fine head," she noted. "Look at that elegant line and those wide-set eyes. This is a real beauty, sir. I hope she travels as well as she looks?"

He smiled down at her indulgently. "Would you like to try her?"

"Oh! May I?" She was quite prepared to tuck her skirts up and canter off, but a glance towards the house dulled her enthusiasm. "I dare not, Barbara would have a conniption. She's already up in arms about Aunt's schemes for us."

"Perhaps another day, then, when the time is more propitious?"

"Oh, yes, please!" She considered. "I must ride over Pentreath in a day or two. I suppose, since you are the vicar, you could not be an improper companion, could you?"

Falsworth agreed that he could not. What a handsome girl she was and how intrigued he would be to see the extent of her holdings. Not much money there, he knew, but with the right management who could tell what might be achieved?

And so that night their dreams were of quite different natures: Lavvy's were of satiny horseflesh, while the vicar dreamed of coronets.

=8=

"AND YOU ALLOWED it, saying nothing? Good heavens, Branston, I had thought better of you!" cried Augusta when she heard of the visit.

The manservant was deferential but unabashed, as befitted an old retainer. "The gentlemen in question, madam, are your lawyer and your vicar."

"God's vicar, perhaps, certainly not mine!" mumbled Lady Augusta.

"Am I to believe, your ladyship, that I was to have forbidden them the hospitality of your home? I am surprised that you think it my place to make such decisions. I am sure I would prefer not to be placed in such a position. Perhaps in future you will be good enough to give me explicit instructions when you are to be absent from home."

"Oh, pshaw!" said the lady in exasperation. "You know perfectly well what I mean and I'll thank you not to wear that plaguey injured expression with me. There are ways of getting around such situations. In the old days at Pentreath you could have done it with a look."

"Pentreath, madam, was a great house."

"And our present domicile is not. Yes, I understand that, but what does it signify? Are you suggesting that standards for one are not standards for the other?"

The manservant looked relieved, as if he had put across a particularly difficult idea. "Exactly, my lady. I am so happy you see my point."

"Well," she conceded, "I daresay a large measure of the fault is mine. I should have insisted they remain at Pecksniff's until I was ready for them in Cheyne Spa."

Branston looked pained at the mention of the watering spot. "And you have not changed your plans, madam?"

Amused and a little uncertain still, she took refuge in an exaggerated vivacity. "Certainly not! I am quite looking forward to having the wickedest den in Wessex. Surely I can count on your goodwill and aid, can I not?"

Branston's equivocal expression sent her into a burst of laughter. "Dear old friend, what a long and varied association we have had. Over the years our lives have altered almost beyond recognition, have they not? But have I yet done anything to bring the slightest stain to the house of Pentreath?"

Chagrin replaced the man's embarrassed look. "Certainly not, madam! I hope you understand that I . . ."

She waved it away. "You did not. You would be incapable of such a lapse."

Branston stood up very stiffly, like a soldier on parade, looking straight ahead. "I should like to assure your ladyship that I . . ."

Sentimentality would soil the moment and she chose irony instead. "Please, Branston, do not let the *gloire* of the situation carry you away."

He shook his head. "Not at all, Lady Augusta. I merely wish to say that I will serve you in any way I can." No matter how I may deplore it, his manner seemed to add, but Lady Augusta skimmed over the ending.

"Very graciously put. I accept. And, now, I think if the tea is ready, I will have it in the small sitting room."

"At once, my lady. And will you have the ginger conserve?"

"Please."

In such small ways are men compromised and women led that one small step closer to ruination.

Unlike other of the more famous watering places, Cheyne Spa has no ancient Brito-Roman heritage nor medieval glory in which to wrap itself. Basically it had always been quite an ordinary English village, rustic and rather backward since Cromwell and the Puritans, until the early part of the eighteenth century when an enterprising promoter capitalised upon the attributes of a natural spring, the waters of which, until then, had been considered unfit for human consumption. Some, having imbibed them, proclaimed that such was still the case, but so clamorous was the public for a watering hole in this part of the world that the (generally apocryphal) claims of the promoter established it as a health center very quickly. Presently, with the blessing and connivance of the then governing corporation, a considerable amount of investment money was procured and a series of elegant, somewhat gimcrack, residential squares and circles were thrown up to accommodate the ever-increasing waves of visitors.

So much for the beginnings. It was the fondness for the place shown by the influential Henrietta Howard, Countess of Suffolk and principal mistress of George II, which set the seal of social approval on the resort, even as Queen Caroline had set her seal upon Henrietta. With the cachet of such royal appreciation the reputation of the spa grew enormous, almost overnight, to rival that of Cheltenham if not of Bath. And if the reputation was somewhat racy (though not excessively so), so much the better. It made for a more relaxed atmosphere than that engendered by its rivals, surely something to be applauded in a resort.

Cheyne had all the usual features: shops, theatres, walks along high ground, static scenic views, a lending library, and, of course, the famous caverns, which lay at just the right distance to provide a pleasant excursion into the countryside. Of all things bright and beautiful nothing had been spared by the hand of the promoter and his followers in the Corporation.

Lady Augusta was gratified to know that Branston was at her back, for she had strongly counted him into her plans for the future. The house she had found was in a quiet cul-de-sac with little frontage but a generous interior, near to the centre of town, and on a level approach. The four major reception rooms were spacious and, if in the day somewhat gloomy of aspect, would brighten considerably under the influence of candlelight and wine. There was an unobtrusive private entrance for the family and another for the servants. The establishment would require careful staffing, for few of the old servants from Pentreath were stylish enough for Cheyne, though cook would be remaining in St. Buryan to keep charge. Augusta would, of course, do the actual interviewing of the new staff, but the screening, and later the training and overseeing of them would fall to the butler. Upon Branston, in fact, would depend the whole tone of the future establishment. It was essential that he be firmly on her side.

She tried not to let the girls see that she herself had nagging doubts. "But what will happen to you, Aunt, if the gamble fails?" Lavvy had asked her only last evening, and she had answered more lightheartedly than she had felt, "I shall live very, *very* carefully in future."

It was all well enough for Lavinia, who would be perfectly content to live in a cottage on the Pentreath grounds. There she would be near her favourite walks along the cliffs and her favourite eyrie above St. Levan's well, where she watched the waves crash against the Vessacks and wondered at the majesty of nature. But Barbara was another thing, and rightly so.

"Why must it be Cheyne, Aunt? What of the continent, where no one knows us. Not France, of course, but there is Baden or . . ."

"You can't find yourself a husband on the continent, if that is what you are thinking," Lavinia interrupted. "Would you really like to be married to someone who wasn't an Englishman? Someone who couldn't even speak your language properly?"

"How do you know he couldn't, or that I should mind that? In any case I should speak to him in French. Miss Gates has seen to that."

"If we must depend upon your knowledge of French," the Countess hooted, "we are all lost indeed!"

Lady Augusta raised her hand in a silencing gesture. "I have consulted with Branston and we agree that . . ."

"Good Lord," said Barbara, still a little put out, "you consulted with a servant, Aunt?"

Lavinia took up the battle at once. "How like you to sneer at Aunt's intentions. For all they taught you at the academy I have always noticed that the good manners didn't take. And, anyway, she was quite right. Branston knows everything!"

She turned back to her aunt. "Where did he suggest? Bath, I'll be bound."

"Why do you not ask him in person?" Lady Augusta replied as the manservant was seen through the doorway going about his work in the adjoining room. Summoned, he shook his head to Lavvy's suggestion.

"Not Bath, your ladyship," he answered. "Too popular by far. So large that perhaps the *best* people are not to be found there at all times. Cheltenham, perhaps, but why travel so far when Cheyne Spa is at hand?"

"The very reason," Barbara complained.

Her aunt froze her with a look. "We leave in two days. And, Branston . . ." her pause was significant ". . . We are *not* at home."

Guiltily the girls left the room, though Branston stayed. Now he raised his eyebrows only very slightly. "To *anyone*, madam? Do you think that wise?"

She considered. "You think I am making too much of it, eh?"

"Perhaps a *little* too much, don't you think, your ladyship? It is not, after all, as if they were mountebanks or ne'er-do-wells, is it?"

"Fudge! I suppose you're right. But I'll have no hanging about, nor languishing nor any of that sort of thing!"

"I hardly think the young ladies would languish, madam."

Her look was one of ill-concealed surprise. "Did I *say* the young ladies? I've seen too often how sentiment takes a middle-aged man in love with a chit. Let them come if they must; better still let them leave their cards and they will be spared a chance of the sharp side of my tongue."

Their ultimate departure was not accomplished without stress, for not only did the Vicar and Young Withering call to make farewells, but it seemed half the district. Not the gentry only, but common folk, especially those who had been in some way connected in the past with Pentreath.

"Somethin' of us goes with yer, mam," said the cobbler gallantly doffing his hat. "Ye'er part 'n parcel of us, m'dear, an' ye'll find ye must come home again at last."

Lady Augusta wept a little at such a speech and wondered what he would say if he knew she considered opening a gambling-parlour. But, she knew, he was right. To be Cornish bred is somehow never to leave Cornwall behind no matter where you go. She would, of course, find she must come home again at last.

=9=

27, Hawk's Lane, Cheyne Spa, Wessex

My dearest brother Jack,

Our journey yesterday went off exceedingly well, though, as usual, Mama fussed about everything in the way she does and was never comfortable for a moment the whole distance. How lucky we had only a few miles to travel. I think you need not have been so taken down by her complaints of the carriage for it is as good-looking as any other I saw on the road, even though it may not have the lines of the latest models. It is in my head that there is something to be said for playing down one's position in life while on the road and, if so, we are well set for transportation.

We arrived at Cheyne Spa to a great din of church-bells, which they say ring for every new batch of travellers. I shudder to think of the effect on the unwell. Fancy some poor wretch dying of an incurable malady only to be constantly cursed by such tintinambulation! I quite shudder.

We found the house after some little trouble, for brother Ralph, who had hired it, had forgotten where it could be found, but, once discovered, all were pleased with his choice except Mama, who complained about everything from the prospect to the inadequate

72

airing of the beds. I rather think she had expected it to be Fogg's Hall miraculously transported to town.

There was a very long list of arrivals here in the newspaper, so that we need not immediately dread absolute solitude, and there is a public breakfast in the lovely St. Gerrans's Gardens, so that we shall not be wholly starved. Mama has bade us all keep our eyes sharp for (as she says) her old friend, the Duke of Towans. What an oddity, do you not think, that we have never before heard of this close connexion with the mighty? I expect inordinate drinking of the waters may have laid him low.

I trust that the trouble with Cleopatra's leg is on the mend. Give her a bit of sugar and say it came from me, then whisper that I shall be home to ride her almost before she misses me. Mama sends love.

Yours affectionately,
Elizabeth Mawson

As well as the unseen duke, they say a Great Person-age has come to Cheyne to lay his heart at the door of his former lady. Can you guess that her initial is F.?

Ever yours,
E.M.

When the Duke of Towans heard the gossip of the proposed visit to the spa of the Prince of Wales, he was deterred from packing his household and moving on only by the memory of his hastily given promise to Lady Augusta. When he said as much to Gerald, the young companion was quite taken aback.

"I had thought you found it congenial hereabout, sir?"

His patron's usually complaisant expression had been replaced by one of profound distaste and it deepened as he explained, "That was before the Fat Florizel arrived." His tone was disgusted. "You will see, my boy, how the very climate of the town will alter the while he is in it. Every respectable person of consequence will of a sudden become a toad-eater and endeavour to crawl upon the shoulders of his neighbour to lift himself to the level of the royal bum." He shuddered realistically, then plaintively added, "And it had promised to be so very pleasant here."

"What I cannot fathom, sir, is why you cherish such an antidote for His Royal Highness? Why, they call him the First Gentleman of Europe, I have heard, and say that he is the very model of what a prince should be. Has he personally injured you in some way, Your Grace?"

The duke smiled a little sadly. "Can one not object to excess upon principle? I am sorry to tarnish your illusions, but the dull fact is that, far from being First Gentleman of anywhere, he is scarcely a gentleman at all. It is hard truth that were he not of the rank he holds, he would be drummed out of virtually every respectable club in London. If ever a bounder was a prince, this one is. As disgusting as a slug, and of even less benefit to the world at large, in my opinion."

"Good Lord, sir, you are talking about the man who is our future sovereign!"

"Aye," Towans agreed, "and the greatest argument toward demolishment of the monarchy." And, like a clock mechanism which, once tightly wound, cannot be stopped again until it has run down, the duke began a recital of social crimes which began with bigamy and ended with infamy.

"I concede that the lady might have been his mistress," Gerald said nervously, "but are you really contending that he *married* Mrs. Fitzherbert when he could not breach her defences in any other way?"

"I am *contending* nothing. I *know* it, told to me from the lips of the lady herself."

"But, Your Grace, what of the Royal Marriage Act?" Gerald knew, as did most of the nation, that no member of the royal family could marry without the express permission of the King, for it had been a much publicized political bone of contention.

"He lied to her," sighed the duke, "and, she, to her sorrow, chose to believe him. It was most unfortunate."

"And you are telling me that, once having *married* her, he grew tired, left her, and *married* again? That he has, in short, *two* wives?" Gerald whistled between his teeth. "Pretty excessive for an English king, what? Even old Harry killed 'em off before taking on the next!"

"Two wives and a mistress between," answered the duke.

"I fear it is no laughing matter, my boy. If only it had ended there, the lady might have recovered with whatever dignity a royal dupe may retain, but, since his official marriage was a gross failure, you may guess what his new measures are."

"You don't mean to say that he has abandoned the Crown Princess in turn?"

"That is old hat. They all but abandoned each other at the altar. If ever there were a marriage of convenience, that one stands near the top of the list! Once the little princess was born they avoided each other as if each were a carrier of the plague.

"No, the bad part is that, having worked his way through the ladies of the court, the Prince has come back to Mrs. Fitz. The poor creature has, decently, taken a vow never to see the blackguard again and flees him frantically, but he follows, never seeming to care what harm he does by his attentions. If he truly loved her, he would allow her her freedom."

"What of his other wife, what does she say of all this?"

"Nothing printable, but, then, she never has. She has borne him an heiress to the crown and that seems to be enough. As I said, they hated each other from the start. He would have sent her home when he first set eyes on her if he could have retained the money Parliament granted him for his marriage. A right profligate is the Prince." His expression lightened for a moment. "I grant you, the Crown Princess *is* a bit eccentric, but so many of that family are that you cannot fault her on that score alone. Too much intermarriage, I daresay. As cousins they may well deserve each other."

"But what of Mrs. Fitzherbert, sir? I understand that she is here, and that is why the Prince has come?"

"I have had intelligence that she is living quietly in Pennyroyal Close, but that, if he continues to impester her, she will not remain there for very long."

Gerald nodded in late-dawning comprehension. "I begin to

see what you aim at, I think. The lady has asked your aid in escaping the attentions of her faithless spouse, but you, on the other hand, have already pledged your backing to the nieces of Lady Augusta, is that it?"

A small square of notepaper drifted to the floor as the duke rose from his chair and began to prowl about the room in a fit of nervous agitation. He did not retrieve it but continued his fulmination as if it had not fallen.

"In a word, yes. You know that I pride myself on keeping aloof from this sort of involvement. I cannot think how I have so entangled myself this time except that Tom Fitzherbert was a great hero of mine in my callow youth. I spent many an illuminating evening among deucedly clever people in their house in Park Street. Now I feel I must help his widow in any way I can."

"Even by putting yourself in the displeasure of the Prince?"

For the first time the duke laughed, though it sounded rather more like a bark. "That is the least of the problem, lad."

As Gerald retrieved the square of notepaper, saw that it was inscribed in an elegant feminine hand, and had his enquiring look met by his friend he had the grace to blush, but the duke understood his curiosity.

"Yes, it *is* from the lady; and, no, you may not from it deduce a romantic attachment, requited or unrequitted, on either side." He put a hand to his head. "I confess, Gerald, that I have no taste for intrigue. I am a simple man, created for the enjoyment of simple pleasures."

"But you feel obliged to be her knight, sir?"

"Lord knows, someone must do it. That royal wretch will hound her to the grave otherwise. I do not wish it, but as a friend I may have little choice."

He rang for his valet and began to dress.

"There is, however, someone with whom I must consult before I continue with this debacle."

— 10 —

IT WAS LATER that same day that Gerald was afforded his first glimpse of 'the royal wretch'.

The afternoon had drifted uneventfully by, for the duke had gone visiting, leaving Gerald to guess where he might be found. The lad surmised that, since his patron had so carefully *not* informed him, it was a likelihood that he was answering the summons of Mrs. Fitzherbert. Certainly Gerald would not be required for that occasion, and since that was the case, he could wander about the spa, indulging in his favorite occupation, watching people.

There are a multitude of ways in which folk pass their personal time. Some cannot be parted from the printed word and will read the fine print of contracts for lack of anything better, others listen to the music that runs through their heads, often tum-ti-tumming away or whistling along with it in a fashion that leads passers-by to stare and smile. Often these personal musicians hum or whistle only the harmony to a tune, which is maddening to everyone else. But people who like to watch other people are in a class by themselves. For one thing they are never bored. Gerald wandered about looking at strangers exactly as if he were at a play, a performance put on for his personal delectation. The exuberance of a small child running wild among his staid elders, the giddy glances a young woman was throwing across the path toward a young man promenading in the opposite direction, three gossiping old ladies reminding him of the legendary norns who had only one eye and one tooth between them, the waspish invalid gentleman who had attendants buzzing about him like flies, all were a source of interest and amusement. He had become so used to the notion that he could see without being seen, that it was quite a shock to suddenly find he was being observed in exactly the same way.

The other watcher was a young woman of perhaps sixteen, not a beauty at all, but pleasant looking, with a sharp face and pert expression which changed rapidly to embarrassment when she found him looking back at her. She dropped her eyes quickly and her blushes were saved by the arrival of another miss of about her own age who was carrying a drawing pad under one arm.

"Lud, Elizabeth, where have you been? Mama is in a pet that you have wandered off all by yourself. Don't you know that young ladies must not be seen on the streets alone? They might be prey to all sorts of immodest proposals!"

Elizabeth involuntarily shot a look Gerald's way and there seemed to be an instant of complicity between them before Hermione dragged her sister back to where Lady Christabel was waiting.

Gerald, out of his vast knowledge of the female species, judged that the girl would be a force to be reckoned with when she had had her *comeout*, probably cut a swathe amongst the young men of her neighbourhood, wherever that might be.

When his grace the duke returned to their rooms it was with a solemn face and so late in the day that they must needs hurry to meet their social obligations. Dressing carefully but quickly, he and Gerald set out for the Assembly.

By the time they reached them, the Upper Rooms were crowded, for the twice-weekly ball was nearly obligatory. Certainly the younger and livelier participants could not have been much pleased by the tedious spectacle of elegant Beau Carlisle leading out one couple of rank after another to dance alone in the center of the floor. Eventually it must seem that the same minuet was danced over and over. No one could guess that this was the night on which all would change.

The duke, constrained as he was, hardly seemed to notice anyone else in the capacious rooms, but Gerald's eyes, as always, darted quickly here and there, seeking out the novel, the celebrated, the influential, or the beautiful. There were precious few in any of the categories. One, however, was the young woman with whom he had exchanged glances a few hours earlier. He tried to do so again, but a discreet buzzing amongst the crowd turned his head toward three new arrivals. Gerald had been introduced to Lady Augusta Mabyn but the young women with her were strangers. One was a handsome creature of perhaps nineteen, decidedly a country woman in the best sense, displaying a golden complexion and hearty good looks. With her was undoubtedly her younger sister, for the family resemblance was strong, but while the first was attractive, this younger one was so exquisitely beautiful that Gerald felt his breath swept quite away. Her complexion, like her sister's, was fresh and unblemished and her hair was of a luxuriant softness that was like a midnight cloud. But it was her eyes which were her prime feature. They were set wide apart under shapely brows and of such a vivid violet hue that they seemed to glow with a banked fire of their own. Gerald did not consider himself unusually susceptible, but in an instant he was in love. Not very deeply, perhaps, nor with anything other than the surface of this heavenly creature. Certainly he was far too level-headed to be swept away by the passion he felt. Perhaps in this he was the most sensible of the young men present, none of whom was immune to Lady Barbara's beauty.

Christabel Mawson, too, was struck by the young woman as the trio entered and was particularly interested in the triple necklace of garnets she was wearing, for she recognised them as the famous Pentreath garnets, valued more for their historical value and antique charm than as gemstones. Long ago she had thought they would some day belong to herself. The older girl was well enough, but, as a countess already, she had little need for looks. Lady Barbara, however, was serious competition for Lady Christabel's own daughters, who stood beside her. There was something *else*, though, about Barbara which teased just at the edge of her mind and danced away just as she thought she knew what it was. Then, glancing beyond the girl, she made the connexion. In the quick flash of memory it all came back to her and she, too, gasped, though it was only secondarily at Barbara's beauty. Instead, it was the combination of Barbara's looks and the distinguished presence of the Duke of Towans standing beyond her. Lady Barbara Pentreath was very nearly the exact image of Jennifer, Duchess of Towans, who had deserted the duke to run off with a tupenny gambler she had met at Bath! Had the duke yet seen the girl?

There was a faint splatter of applause as Beau Carlisle, Master of Ceremonies, resplendent in orchid satin, led out into the centre the Great Personage of whom all had come to catch a glimpse. As the Prince of Wales stepped out there was a long, low sigh from the spectators, a sound somewhere between admiration and longing, for the Prince was, after all, the visible representative of royal favour. The King's eldest son was an impressive sight for all his corpulence, since he moved with great dignity abetted by his height and air of personal consequence. It was a pleasant visage, though the pouting lips and retroussé nose forced upon him something of the look of a woman *en travesti*. He looked about him affably and a little complacently as Carlisle crossed the circle of floor and drew from a retiring corner the ancient Duchess of Doddington, for ritual prescribed that a ball be opened by the gentleman and lady of the highest rank present.

The Ceremonial Master pounded thrice with the metal heel of his staff of office and the dancing began.

Prince George stepped out the obligatory minuet with the duchess to the muted chorus of creaking stays—none could say whether they were hers or his. His glance, though, was restless. Clearly he was not enamoured of his partner. Protocol demanded that he tread the steps with his lady a second time, but, later, several of the spectators declared they knew the exact moment of the social revolution. His roving look may have been seeking a glimpse of his elusive lover, but it fell upon another enchanting visage and lingered there. The Prince knew a good thing when he saw it and was never afraid to seize the moment.

When the stately measures were concluded the King's son

dropped a deep and elegant bow to his elderly partner and, as she was gathering for a second go, handed her back to Carlisle. Without unseemly haste, he made directly for Lady Augusta Mabyn and her wards, Carlisle quickstepping ahead of him.

"Your Royal Highness," intoned Beau, "may I present the Lady Augusta Mabyn, her niece, the Countess of Pentreath, and Lady Barbara Pentreath."

The trio curtsied, His Royal Highness bowed, Carlisle hovered in agitation, and revelation struck the Duke of Towans like a blow. From where he was standing, both the Beau and Augusta's youngest girl were in his direct line of vision. The floodgates of memory opened and unhappy recollection washed through. How very incredibly like Jennifer the girl was. And her juxtaposition with Carlisle resolved at once the nagging question of the man's past. His name was not the same, but the blackguard had not changed *all* out of countenance. Towans had seen this cicisbeo mincing his way about the town all the days he had been here, had been disconcerted by the faint sense of *deja vu* when in his presence. Now he recognised him. Now he knew. And Carlisle, inadvertantly meeting his eyes, knew that he knew. And trembled.

All social traditions come at last to dust and the Prince of Wales broke this outmoded one of rank dancing exclusively with rank by leading out the Lady Barbara Pentreath (with Lady Augusta's permission). The Duke of Towans shattered it forever by immediately following with the young woman's aunt, sharing the floor with royalty, a thing unheard of. All happening so quickly as to seem prearranged. The eyes of England, personified by the denizens of Cheyne Spa, were upon them and upon Carlisle, the social arbiter. The master of spa-manners who dared not gainsay either the Prince or the duke.

Those whose memory was long and saw the connexion Lady Christabel had seen watched with closeheld breath. The remainder, washed in a reflected glory, merely saw in it the spectacle of the great indulging their greatness.

In a generation it would seem such a trifle. Two exalted couples enacting a social transformation with stately grace. It would give the gossips and the gazettes something to worry for weeks and the social historians would class it with Edward III and the story of the garter as a transition point. If the Prince was at all surprised at the turn of things, he disclosed it by not the turn of a hair. He was, after all, still and always, the centrepiece of the evening, which was where he chose to be. He had not found the lady for whom he had come to Cheyne Spa, but the young woman with whom he was dancing was ravishing. He might go away again in a day or a week, but he knew the temper of the people around him and they would cherish this evening forever. What a benison it was to give them pleasure.

Lady Christabel watched these unorthodox proceedings with a careful eye, judging how it might be turned to her advantage and knowing that, just by having been present this evening, she was thrust into the forefront of fashion.

Her son Ralph, beside her, alternately blushed and paled at the vision of Barbara, whom he had quite forgotten for the better part of six months. His *tendre*, he found, remained.

Hermione swayed and jiggled in time to the music while Elizabeth watched them all, locking it away in her brain and sealing it with a wry smile far in advance of her age.

= 11 =

COOL TONES OF sea-green and blue prevailed in the sitting-room into which the parlourmaid ushered the Duke of Towans next morning. It was a hired house, of course, but above that it had been kept, perhaps deliberately, as impersonal as it was possible to be. No bibelots, no small personal touches softened the room. It was as if the tenant had consciously studied for dissociation, had wanted a total absence of distraction and evaded even normal intercourse with the world.

The only intrusion upon this impersonality was the portrait of a lady which hung above the mantel, a prim and fiercely virtuous woman of middle years. Romney, by the look of it, thought the duke, but puzzlingly done considerably more in the manner of his masculine portraits than the usually softer and more facile feminine ones.

Towans himself, when a young boy, had once been painted by Romney and he recalled the experience with a mixture of impatience for the conventions which had required it and affection for the painter himself with whom he had got on well. But, Lud! what a tedious penance it had been for a young lad to stifle inside during a fine summer when he would rather by far have been with the stableboy catching coneys in the hedgerows than sitting for a portrait as the young heir. Later, of course, the painter had gone in for larger, often literary subjects such as *Milton and His Daughters* and the handsome *A Scene From 'The Tempest'* which he had painted for Boydell's Shakespeare Gallery, but their friendship had continued over the years and it was difficult for Towans to imagine how the artist had come to see Mrs. Fitz in this aspect of grim determination.

The woman in the painting had a face too heavy for beauty, a nose too aquiline and a chin far too determined, but when the original of it entered the room and held out her hands to her visitor, it was evident that no mere painting could capture the air of freshness and charm which emanated from her. Her large, expressive eyes were probably called hazel by some but in reality they were a rich, golden topaz. They were, however, troubled.

"It is true, then?" she asked. "He has found me again?"

The duke nodded. "You were wise to avoid the assembly." He looked at her narrowly, detecting something in her manner. "But I am telling you nothing? You already have intelligence of it? Were you a little mouse in the corner?"

She had the grace to blush. "My maid, Miranda, served as my eyes. Well, why not? He's set his spies on me for years. I only return the compliment. I believe the young woman to whom he paid his address was very beautiful?"

"So she was," Towans replied without enthusiasm. Then, curiously, "How long has it been since you have seen him?"

"Nearly four years since we parted, except for . . ." She hesitated.

"Yes?"

Mrs. Fitzherbert flushed. "Just before his marriage . . . about two days before . . ." She said, "I looked out of the window where I was living in Richmond and saw a horse and rider cantering back and forth through the trees of the park."

"You are sure it was he?"

"Quite sure. He made himself conspicuous enough, riding back and forth, back and forth, and then around the fields surrounding the house."

"And you . . . what did you do?"

"Nothing. I knew what it would mean. When dusk fell he went away. To the arms of Lady Jersey, I don't doubt, to draw strength for his ordeal."

Towans sighed. "How you must hate the Princess for her part in all this."

"Caroline? Poor thing, not at all. He has treated her far worse than any of us and, still, she has somehow fulfilled her purpose and given him an heiress, that counts for something."

"What little comfort you have, my lady," he commiserated with her. "Are you, do you think, fortunate that there were no children from your marriage?" And, as he said it, he saw an odd look pass over the face of the Prince's wife.

"As a Catholic in England," she said a little sharply, "I have grown accustomed to small comfort. As for children, they would have been, perhaps, illegal but certainly not illegitimate. I was married in the church and nothing can change my status in the eyes of God."

"Madame," he said hurriedly, "please believe that I did not mean to . . ." She laid her hand on his arm.

"No, of course not, my friend. I know that. I am grateful and will be grateful any help you can give me in this matter."

"What is it, exactly, that you have in mind?"

"I am so tired, Towans. I am tired of flight, of dissimulation. I want you to talk to him. Settle my future."

The duke all but reeled in surprise. "My God, madam you ask much of friendship. I have made so little secret of my antipathy for your husband that, surely, you could find a better mediator."

"I do not know of a better," she answered.

"I am likely to do your cause more harm than good. I am no great hand at diplomacy, you know."

Mrs. Fitzherbert smiled sadly. "I trust your judgement and I know you are a gentleman."

"Quite honestly . . ." he began, but she held up a staying hand.

"Please. I know your sentiments. That is why you are the finest choice for the mission. As a gentleman you will hold your views in check, but they will always be there, modifying your attitude of the moment. You will not be swayed by his charm."

"He has none for me, I fear. I wish I could say otherwise."

"I think you misjudge him a little. He is spoiled and willful, I know, but he is not a monster like some of his kin."

"He has wounded you often, madam, and without provocation. No man could be a good one and guilty of that crime. It is beyond me why you defend him, at least to me of all people."

"You really do not know? Then you really do not know me."

"I confess that your reasons are unfathomable."

"They are simple," said Mrs. Fitzherbert. "In the eyes of God and my church he is my husband. And a second reason, if one is needed: I love him. Are we women not foolish in our loyalty? Despite everything he has done and not done, I love."

The duke set his jaw against saying more, for, no matter how foolish he felt her reasons to be, he respected this woman.

"It's against my better judgement, you know."

"I appreciate that. You'll do it, then?"

The duke shrugged uncomfortably. "I make no promises. I will attempt to see him, but if he . . ."

"He will see you if he knows you come from me."

The duke looked at her levelly. "I must say, madam, that you confuse me. You have never made it clear to me what you hope for in this. What is it you want from it, from me? It would help me to know before I talk to the Prince."

"I cannot tell you that," said Mrs. Fitzherbert, "because I do not at all know myself how I feel or what I want. It seems to change from moment to moment. I think I could live a quiet, comfortable life with no regrets, if he would leave me alone."

"You do not want him back, then? You are sure of that?"

She lifted her chin and looked him straight in the eye. "Oh, no, I do not want him back. I could not return to that life. The strain would be more than I could bear.

"Oh, no, I do not want him back. Please believe me in this."

The duke bowed over her hand.

She had convinced him at last.

= 12 =

LOOKING BACK UPON the events of the previous evening, Gerald somehow felt that, rather than marking it as having provided his first glimpse of the Prince of Wales, it would necessarily be enshrined as the date of the first time he saw Lady Barbara Pentreath. There was, he knew himself well enough to recognise, a certain amount of infatuation present in his excitement, but it had to do with the recognition of someone extraordinary in the extreme. He knew enough of the world from his association with the duke to be certain that, should Lady Barbara marry into the high London circles to which she aspired, she would have entered her own milieu among the beauties and beaus of Whig society. Hers was that fashionable sort of beauty that would make people stand upon their chairs to ogle her across a crowd. Certainly to have been taken up by Prinny, however briefly, would scarcely stand in her way.

Despite the girl's youth, Gerald sensed that within Lady Barbara there was a kind of *presence* working, a natural self-will that would always work in her favour, assuming it was not thwarted by an ill-made marriage to some country dullard. Not particularly clever herself, Gerald suspected, Lady Barbara would need a strong and clever husband, probably older and already established in the world, to show her to her best advantage.

As to the rest of the evening, Gerald had found little of which to take note. The attention of the Prince to Lady Barbara had been the event of the most overt interest, and the request of His Royal Highness that the quintet of musicians play an example of that new London sensation, the waltz, the most significant. The waltz allowed, if not demanded, the presence of more than one or two couples on the floor and the spectators were quick to follow the lead of His Highness and make an effort, however halting, to master the unfamiliar step and rhythm. Not all had been drawn in, of course. The outraged Duchess of Doddington had stood aside in stiff-necked disapproval, though, surprisingly, the vanguard had been headed by Lady Augusta's cousin, Lady Christabel, who thrust herself into the fore with an alacrity that suggested a certain rivalry between them.

When the ball was over there was a general departure and then a stealthy return to the gaming in the Lower Rooms. Lady Christabel made her appearance there as well, though it was obvious she was a novice at both barrow and verté, for when the wooden sleeve came round to her she had no notion how to release the card. When she moved to the faro table she proved more successful, if conservative, by removing her winnings after each *coup*, leaving only the sum she had first ventured. Gerald saw that at another table Ralph, the young man he took to be her son, was once again playing against the man Filer. From his expression he seemed not to be winning.

Thinking back to the ball, Gerald could not recall Lady Augusta and her nieces after the interval, though he remembered that the Countess Lavinia had seemed equally as popular as her stunning sister. Perhaps, in fact, all the very young women had been sent away, for the Mawson girls, too, were absent from his memories of the later evening. He wondered what that sharp-faced chit might have made of the spectacle of her mother avidly wagering at the faro table?

Lady Christabel, though she felt obliged to profess satiety to her family, was quite satisfied with the recollection of the evening. Not only had she recalled herself to the duke and reforged old connexions, learnt how to waltz and discovered she had an aptitude for it, but even managed to speak to Augusta without overt rancour, even though it was quite disgusting how the woman thrust those nieces forward. (Not that the youngest *needed* to be thrust anywhere, being quite forward enough on her own account.)

The highlight, of course, was having been presented to the Prince of Wales in an informal setting, quite a feather in any woman's crown. She had been presented at court, years ago, but that was quite a different thing. She had her old associations with the duke to thank for the presentation; Augusta would never have lifted a finger. After Lady Barbara had been taken up by His Highness and the duke swept Augusta onto the floor in that *peculiar* fashion, there had been of necessity a few minutes of chat with His Highness when the dance had done. Augusta would have ignored her, but not Towans, who had looked her way and signalled with his eyes that she should draw nearer. She was quite certain of that. The Prince had been condescension itself—so affable—quite, quite charming—and Christabel had basked in the afterglow for hours. Even now it brought a blush of pleasure to her cheek. Elizabeth, of course, had something spiteful to say, but that was her usual manner. Hermione, however, had been a disgrace, complaining right up until supper because she, too, had not been drawn into the Royal Presence. Christabel had finally been obliged to send both gels back to their rooms with a few timely words on proper public behaviour. What a pity dear Ralph had not been near enough to be included. It would do him a world of good to be known by the Prince. Well, there was time still, time enough. They were all saying that His Royal Highness would remain in Cheyne Spa as long as Mrs. Fitzherbert did.

Elizabeth poked her head into the room and smiled as if butter wouldn't melt in her mouth. And after being so rude last evening about her introduction to the Prince.

"I'm just going down to the lending library, Mama. Can I bring you anything when I come back?"

"Not alone, I hope?" Lady Christabel asked severely. "Where is your sister?"

"No, no. Hermione is going with me. She finds she needs a new drawing pencil. The one she brought is too hard, she says. And Ralph will be with us, so we'll be quite safe."

Lady Christabel delicately touched her temples with Cologne water. "Very well, Eliza. Run along. I shall just rest this afternoon, I think."

Why was Elizabeth smiling in that disagreeable way? "The social life *is* exhausting, isn't it, Mama? Shall you be well enough for the concert tonight, do you think?"

Lady Christabel waved her out in a languid way. "We shall see, my child. Run along now. Keep close to your brother and for heaven's sake keep track of Hermione. She is such a ninny-hammer since we've arrived. I cannot think what has come over her."

"Probably the excitement, Mama," suggested Eliza. "I, for one, had never thought the Great World would be quite like this."

Nor did I, thought Lady Christabel happily.

And that scapegrace, Ralph, teaching his own mother to be a gamester! Though, really, there was nothing to it if you kept your wits about you. She would, she knew, prove this thesis this evening when the gambling recommenced after the concert.

Which raised another question: To attend the concert or not to attend the concert? Faltenelli was long past his prime, they all said, but she had never heard a male soprano. It could be a novel experience. But she was still undecided about allowing the girls to be exposed to such influences. He was a *castrato*, after all, and it hardly seemed proper. Hermione was especially impressionable.

Later, of course, the gaming. She felt a delicious thrill of anticipation.

Lady Barbara, for her part, thought the evening unequalled. Never mind that Aunt Augusta had dragged them away directly after supper. She, Barbara Pentreath, had been shown singular attention by the Prince of Wales! Nothing could ever be the same again. Never mind that Aunt Augusta was contemplating a social gaffe and that it was Lavinia who had inherited the title and didn't give a snap for it, Barbara had danced with the Prince of Wales who, though he might be plump and rather inclined to pump and puff, was still the Prince of Wales! It was amusing, too, how the duke had been so jealous of the attention that he led her own aunt out upon the floor in competition. How transparent! Barbara was accustomed to men being struck by her beauty and took it rather for granted, but a duke was decidedly different! Especially this one. Rich as Croesus, handsome still, and just enough older to make an indulgent husband for a young and beautiful wife. Being a duchess would offer so many opportunities.

It was odd, but Aunt Augusta was being decidedly peculiar about allowing her wards to mingle with the gamesters in the Lower Rooms.

"You're worried about being a shill for my little games at home, Barbara. Then you must stay away from the tables altogether."

"Oh, but, Aunt . . ."

"No, no, my dear. You must avoid even the faintest suggestion of impropriety. Since last evening, Barbara, you must be far above the slightest criticism. You are in a dangerous place, having reached a great height much too soon. We must be very careful. I have my doubts even about the Faltenelli concert."

Lavvy looked at her strangely. "I had thought, Aunt, that you were a great admirer of Faltenelli? Lord knows, I shall not mind staying away, but you?"

Lady Augusta, who was being extraordinarily patient with both of them, favoured her with the sweetest and gentlest of smiles. "I *am* his admirer, my dearest, no one more so. I remember him as he *was*." There was a brief silence as if she were communing with some distant past. Then, briskly, she added, "But I am not a young gel who has yet to have her comeout. We cannot be too careful."

But at Barbara's smothered cry of protest, she relented. "Perhaps in the interests of education we can waive the conventional logic, eh? You may never hear his like again. Think what you can tell your grandchildren!"

Somehow Barbara felt she had been scored upon, but she was not sure exactly how it had happened. At any rate the duke was certain to be in attendance at the concert.

Beau Carlisle's arm, moving out across the top of the dressing table, overturned the bottle and the raw smell of gin quickly pervaded the room. Slowly he raised his head, despite the roaring agony of it, and stared at himself in the glass. Who was this stranger, this raddled old man with red creases across his face where he had slept against his sleeve? Some ageing, defeated stranger come at last to the end of his road.

It had been an uneasy life and the past night had been the worst of it. When that girl had walked in with Lady Augusta, the spit of Jenny Towans, and when he and the duke had seen her both at the same time . . . Lud! That was a moment he'd not care to live again. 'If I'd had the strength of me legs,' he thought, 'I'd have cut and run.'

Splashing water on his face, he hawked, clearing his throat. Gad, he could spit sixpences! Perhaps another little swallow of gin to clear his head? Damn the luck! Just when he's made himself a neat little nest here and was like to put enough by to support his senility. And damn the duke! Why couldn't he have gone to Bath or Cheltenham like the rest of his kind? Damn them all! Damn itchy Jennifer, a draggle-tailed slut if there ever was one, for all her being the Duchess of Towans! But most of all, damn his own eyes, for being such an arrant fool!

Still, that had been a long time since. He had lived for years with the threat of discovery hanging over his head and now the end of it was come. He wasn't sure but what he was glad of it. Ruined or not, the pressure would be gone.

Thoughtlessly he stripped the frowsty garments from his body and immersed his entire head in the water, coming up spluttering and shaking water about the room without regard for anything in it. Not that there was aught of value. His life was not lived here but in the Assembly building, the Upper Rooms and the Lower Rooms to which the dual aspects of his life were relegated. On the one level he was the social arbiter, the psychopomp who led them through the phases of their lives, and on the other level he was the banker who emptied their pockets to his own advantage. Surely, there was a lesson here. Perhaps even a way out.

It might be inevitable that he must vacate Cheyne Spa, but what oracle had decreed that he must go empty handed?

= 13 =

WHEN THE DUKE asked Gerald to carry a message to the hotel where the Prince and his suite were quartered, rather than sending it in the ordinary way, the young man knew that something momentous was in the wind and suspected that it had to do with the Prince's unfortunate wife . . . or rather, his original wife . . . Mrs. Fitzherbert. But try as he might, there was no way he could know, however, what the message contained. He had to be content with being shown by a flunkey to the Prince's apartments, there to deliver his message to the equerry and wait for a reply. He considered himself fortunate that he need not cool his heels in the hall as the flunkey who accompanied him must do, but was put in a rather pleasant little sitting room where he quietly contemplated the crown of his hat and mused upon the probable nature of his mission. He had not expected to divine it from such a prominent source.

The Prince of Wales, when he strode into the room, was garbed in a loose paisley robe and a tasselled Turkish cap set sideways across his curls. Out of his stays he was ample in girth, yet in some fashion, Gerald felt, more impressive than in his public turnout. He had the duke's message in his hand and was waving it wildly as he crossed the room to where Gerald was sitting.

"What does he want, eh? Tell me that. She's put him up to this, whatever it is, eh? What the devil does she mean by refusing to see me? Does she take me for a fool? That I do not know where she is living? I *have* an intelligence service, after all, what?"

Gerald scrambled hastily to his feet. "I beg Your Royal Highness's pardon, but I . . ."

"Well," cried the Prince, his face nearly apoplectic, "he don't fool me, eh? You've got to get up demmed early indeed to fox me in that way. Begs me the favour of a meeting, does he? A private affair between gentlemen, he says. Oh yes, I know what he says about me in the circle of his so-called friends. I have an intelligence service, as I say. Tell me every demmed thing, whether it is relevant or not." He perused the letter again. "What the devil does he mean, the ambiguous lout? A private affair between gentlemen, faugh! I cannot tell whether he is requesting an audience or calling me out!"

Gerald was aghast. "Oh, sir! That is, Your Royal Highness . . . I am certain, sir, that the duke had no intention of calling you out!"

The Prince surveyed him pessimistically. "Harrumph! Don't think he meant that, eh? Yes. I can see that. You'd be a bit young to be his second, wouldn't you? Eh?" He peered at Gerald closely through his quizzing glass. "Dammee, I know you, don't I? Seen you recently, I'd swear. Who the devil are you, boy?"

"Gerald Wetherbridge, sir." Bowing slightly. "You may have seen me at the ball last evening."

"Eh, the ball? Ah, yes, you were with Towans. I confess I remember mostly a raving beauty of a gel, not you. No offence."

"None taken, sir. That would be the Lady Barbara Pentreath."

"Yes, I know that. Lady Augusta's ward. Fine looking piece. A mere child, but a true beauty nonetheless." He peered at Gerald again. "You are to Towans . . . what?"

The lad hardly knew how to answer. Secretary? Companion? Messenger? "He and my father were close friends, sir."

"Wetherbridge . . . Wetherbridge . . . a member from Wessex, was he? Passed on a year or two ago?"

"Yes, sir, that was my father. He died five years ago come Michaelmas."

The Prince was ruminative. "I remember him. Demmed Tory rascal. Caused me no end of trouble in Parliament about my finances. Seemed to think a prince can live on air." Then the sky cleared and he began to radiate bonhomie. "But that's no fault of yours, eh? Well then, take this answer back to your . . ." He looked at Gerald again, very closely. "I say, he isn't your . . . ah . . . what I mean is . . . you're not his . . .?"

"No, Your Highness," Gerald assured him. "He was my father's friend."

"Hmph, yes. Well, be that as it may be. Though I have known friends who . . . still, never mind that. Say to the duke that I shall be happy to see him on any matter whatsoever and inquire if tomorrow before noon will be convenient?"

"I am sure it will be, sir.

"Are you? We shall see." But it was said without rancour. "Demmed good tailor you have. Rare to see a chap like you, at your age, so well fitted."

"The duke's tailor, sir."

"Oh. Well, yes. I suppose." He seemed to have run out of all that excessive energy and sat down, puffing slightly. "Bad for m'health all that overexcitement, you know."

Casually he flicked snuff onto his thumb, inhaled it and threw up his handkerchief to catch the sneeze. "Now, young man, what is this all about?"

Gerald could only tell the truth. "I have no idea, sir. The duke did not discuss it with me."

"But he *has* seen Mrs. Fitzherbert?"

"I believe so, sir."

"You think she really wants to be shut of me? It couldn't be true, could it? Must be a ploy. She always did know how to catch my attention. What do you think, eh?"

Gerald felt quite sorry for this odd man, his future king.

"I *am* sorry, sir. I honestly don't know."

The Prince stared disconsolately off into space. "No, no of course there is no reason you should know. Tell him tomorrow, eh? I'll see him tomorrow."

When Gerald backed gingerly out of the room the Prince was still staring into space.

"Well," asked the duke when his messenger returned with the Prince's answer, "how did you find him when out of the public gaze?"

Gerald took a moment to consider. "Actually, Your Grace, I rather liked him. He can be very engaging."

The duke nodded agreement. "There's a great deal of charm there, but it is dangerous to believe too deeply in it. You cannot live a life on charm alone, much less reign over a country."

— 14 —

THE CONCERT WAS a success only in the sense of historical perspective, Lady Augusta was saddened to find. Faltinelli's voice, once a glorious instrument, was worn to a mere shadow of itself. She was sorry to think of those in the audience who would go away believing that this was all that had ever been.

She said as much to the duke as they were chatting at the interval. "I pray that when my time has come I shall have the wisdom to step gracefully into obscurity."

Her companion appeared to be more than a little annoyed. "That, madam, is bosh," he said rather rudely. "If Faltinelli's voice has faded he has made up a great deal of the lack with his exquisite technique and execution. As with a woman, it seems to me. The situation is much the same. There is beauty in every age if one has the perspicacity to find it." He gestured across the room to where two elderly women stood in conversation. One was the Duchess of Doddington, her face leaded and painted with an unhealthy flush upon the cheeks, the other a lady of about the same age, elegantly but simply gowned. Eschewing the elaborate flounces and maquillage of her friend, she was, without effort, one of the attractions in the room, clear-eyed and with a face which betrayed, not so much a coming-to-the-end-of life, but a life well and fully lived.

"Which would you choose to be, Lady Augusta?" asked the duke. "You are young enough, I daresay, to choose either."

Very near them in the other direction, the two Pentreath sisters stood surrounded by their individual courts of admirers.

Barbara seemed quite in her element, flirting and fluttering her fan, shooting quick glances from her incredible violet eyes, glances that evidently struck like darts straight to the hearts of her swains. Lavinia's forte seemed to be warmth and honesty and if her suitors were less love-struck, they also seemed more sincere. Lady Barbara caught the eyes of her aunt and the duke on her and flashed them a winning smile.

"She admires you greatly," said Lady Augusta. "I believe you are her beau ideal."

The duke, thinking of his late wife, shivered involuntarily. It was a response of that odd kind that is described as someone walking over one's grave. "Do you remember my duchess at all?" he asked Lady Augusta.

Augusta, whose recollection was only of someone very young and rather shallow, shook her head. "I don't think I could have seen her more than once or twice."

"She was very like your Barbara." It was said not unkindly, but with enough point that Lady Augusta immediately took his meaning.

"She is very fond of you all the same," she said. "You may chastize me for prying, but is there a woman in your life at all? Or have you become that sort of man who needs no softer influence?"

The duke's smile, wry though it was, absolved her of indelicacy. "Are you asking, Lady Augusta, if I keep a mistress?"

"I wouldn't go so far, but . . ."

He laughed almost out loud; audibly enough, at any rate, so that those nearby turned. "You are quite an outrageous woman, Augusta," he said in a lower tone. "I had forgotton how downright inquisitive you could be when we were children. But, to answer you, no, I have neither an *amie* nor a mistress, nor a 'special friend', nor any woman closer to me than my cook.

"And the more I see of society, the more likely I am to stay in that condition."

"Nonsense," said Lady Augusta, "you exhibit all the earmarks of a man ready at any moment to take the fall. And quite rightly, too. I have no patience with men who think they are too good for ordinary life."

He seemed surprised. "Do I appear that way to you? As priggish as that?"

"Have I found the chink in your armour? What do you care what I think, if you need no feminine influences in your life? I am sure you do very well amongst cigars and port and bawdy stories. The company of your peers is undoubtedly exactly what you crave and thrive upon.

"But do not be too smug, my friend. You are like a ripe apple on the tree. One of these days a pretty young woman will beckon and you will fall off your limb directly into her lap. I hope I shall be there to see it."

He pulled a long face. "It is no good, Augusta. I am not in the market for your nieces. I've had one quite like Barbara and what a pity it would be if Lavinia's title went to waste."

She slapped him quite hard on the wrist with her folded fan.

"Do not take too many liberties, madam," he warned.

"I had rather it were your head, wretch," she said in a quite unladylike growl and his fox's bark of laughter made the heads turn again. Including that of Lady Christabel.

She had been regarding them for some minutes, looking away from time to time only to keep an eye on her three children. Hermione was being held in conversation by a sallow youth with large, soulful eyes and a skin problem which betrayed his age, and Elizabeth was, in her usual way, standing back and watching everyone else. Only Ralph was out of sight and she soon discovered him amongst the crowd about Lady Barbara.

Turning her attention back to Cousin Augusta and the duke, she speculated silently on their relationship. Was it deeper than it seemed? They appeared to be very intimate. Could it be that Augusta, herself, had designs on the duke? It was not unheard of that silly women should throw themselves at the head of any eligible man. But, my word, if she succeeded, think how insupportable she would be. And what an advantage to marrying off those girls.

Ralph's slightly braying laughter among the crowd of Barbara's admirers returned him to his mother's mind and she, catching his eye, summoned him with a look. He came reluctantly.

"Could you not spend some time with your mother, dear, rather than leaving her all alone in this crush?"

The look of anguish he directed toward Lady Barbara was not lost on his mother. "I really do not think you should waste your time panting after that heart," she said kindly. "If you must pursue such a course it might better be with Lavinia. She, at least, will bring a title to her husband."

"Not to her *husband*, Mama," Ralph contradicted, "only to their children. Besides, quite honestly, she has no conversation. All she can talk about is dog and horses and how wonderful it is to be out of doors. Not my sort at all. We should never agree."

Then he brightened. "What a pity Jack isn't here."

What meant that sudden glint in his mother's eye?

During the second part of the concert Lady Augusta had time to reflect upon the duke's sentiments concerning age and maturing. As she listened to Faltinelli's peerless rendition of a lovely aria from Gluck's *Orféo ed Euridice* her heart seemed to long for things set aside for many years.

> *Che farò senza Euridice?*
> *Dove andrò senza il mio ben?*

> What shall I do without Eurydice?
> Where shall I go without my treasure?

Drat Towans! thought Augusta. Why cannot he merely make light conversation like other people, rather than causing one to recollect?

"Euridice!" cried Faltinelli. "Euridice!"

Augusta had first heard the opera in Paris shortly after she had been married. The Orpheus had been a tenor rather than a male contralto and the words in French rather than Italian, but the sentiments had been the same and the music as exquisitely beautiful as now. She had thought then that happiness would go on forever and ever. She had no premonition of how soon she would be a widow.

>*Si, aspetta, o cara ombra dell idol mio!*
>*Aspetta!*

>Wait, sweet paragon shadow.
>Wait.

Yes, the voice was faded. But there was a purity she had not heard before, a level of existence, a nuance which had gone unnoticed.

"*Aspetta*," she whispered to herself. "Wait." Furtively she dabbed at her eyes with a crumpled handkerchief. She felt quite melancholy at the moment, but also, somehow, very much alive. How could that be?

$=\mathbf{15}=$

LADY CHRISTABEL WENT down to the Lower Rooms on the arm of her son, Ralph, with a distinct shiver of anticipation. It was not the prospect of winning a great deal of money which attracted her as . . . what? . . . something secret, something forbidden. And it was a kind of contest, was it not? The triumph of winning against the house, against the odds.

The Lower Rooms of the Assembly were not as extensive as those grander ones above because a portion of the space was set aside for utilitarian purposes, but the area remaining had been used well. Made into a pair of spacious chambers connected by an arched doorway, they were crowded with all the usual games of chance. As well as single tables of barrow and verté there were two or more each of hazard, whist and E.O., as well as Beau Carlisle's famous faro game, which had gone on uninterruptedly for nearly a decade. The gamesters ranged from the timid tyros to the old and jaded tricksters like Filer, from the affluent who played with a kind of careless élan to those whose very future depended upon the turn of a card. The ordinary incident of an evening in the Lower Rooms, the losing of an odd thousand, attracted very little notice. Coolness and massive imperturbability were what was wanted. And, for the most part received, though the frenzy of losers sometimes took astonishing forms. A man who had often plunged above his head was complimented upon his nonchalance at repeated losses and in reply opened his shirt and disclosed his breast all lacerated by his own fingernails. In the other direction is the story of a fortunate player who, when he realised a large winning, went straightaway from the rooms. Next day he made the wisest provisions of any gambler since the beginning of time: he arranged for food, clothing, washing and lodging for the next ten years in order to look forward to that long a period of play undisturbed by any anxiety.

Lady Augusta Mabyn was already in the gambling area, not playing but walking about and peering at the games in progress in a penetrating way.

"Ah, there you are, Christabel," she greeted her cousin. "Come to pay your tuppence, have you? Have a care you do not fly too high. You have an example to set to your family, after all."

Lady Christabel took this in surprisingly good part. "I believe I am quite a *rara avis* in these parts," she laughed. "I honestly come to play for the sport rather than for the winning. Not but what I pick my pennies off the table, you understand. My boy, Ralph, over there, has not the temperament, I fear. I see him go quite pale at the prospect of losing.

"But you don't seem to play at all, Augusta?" she added.

Lady Augusta replied with all the surface refinements of geniality. "I derive all my pleasure from the success of others. One learns so much by merely observing, don't you think?"

"No," said Lady Christabel, "I prefer to play."

As we have seen, it was faro which enflamed Lady C. and it was to this table to which she almost immediately made her way. Tonight she did not even hesitate nor take a breath before she flung herself into the play.

Faro is a round game of cards played between the keeper of the bank and as many as could crowd about the table. Like the children's game of Self and Company, which it recalls, it is simple in the extreme, appealing most strongly perhaps to those who do not require the complex ramifications of skill and daring to make their mark.

Each bettor places his stake on any of the thirteen cards from ace to king and when the amounts have been set throughout the company, the dealer takes a full pack of cards and deals it in pairs into two piles, one to either hand. On the cards falling to the right hand he *pays* the stakes, on those which fall on to the left pile he *takes* the stakes. The bare bones of this sound quite ridiculous, but, in fact, there was hardly a dull moment, for the game was full of incident, with no long pauses for shuffling and dealing. That was what endeared it to those, like Lady Christabel, of limited skill and experience.

This same lack of experience and skill served to diffuse another fact: that it is impossible in the long run to win. The odds are tremendously in favour of the dealer. Not only does he claim all ties when the same card appears on both heaps, but also the last card but one delivers its stakes to him upon whichever hand it falls, and there is as well a certain impalpable but very real 'pull of the table' which operates in his favour. These hidden assests are what had kept Carlisle in business for so many years. On a bad night he might lose heavily, but it was restored with interest within a week.

Lady Christabel laid her stake on the queen for luck and was at once rewarded. After this first *coup* she removed her winnings just as she had done the night before, but that was, after all, the tame way to play and she had expectations of becoming a flyer. So the next time, having regained her original stake, she let the money ride . . . and ride again . . . and still another *coup*. Encouraged by her run of luck, and by the attention she received from the other players, and by her own rush of curiosity as to how long this stake could build, she let it go again, recklessly. Even if she lost she would be losing nothing of what she had had when she came down into the Lower Rooms, since she had already recovered her original stake. She might have reached the fabled *soixante et le va* and claimed sixty-three times the original stake, but she found the excitement too intoxicating. The pressure was almost intolerable. She would stop now, she thought, because she was not yet ready for such heights.

But before she could withdraw, the faithless queen showed her face simultaneously on both piles and her winnings had all vanished. A substantial amount it was by then, too. There was a low moan of commiseration around the table, but Christabel smiled brightly and shrugged. Then she turned away from the table, leaving her original stake as a tip for Carlisle.

There was a ripple of applause as she walked away and she squared her shoulders in appreciation of it. So this was how people behaved in the Great World. And this was only a small second-rate spa. What must it be like in London now? She had had her season there, but it had been so long ago, and she had been far too young to enjoy it.

She drifted through the arch into the other room to where her son was at the hazard table with Mr. Filer. The youth looked up with a degree of apprehension when she came over to them. His knuckles were white from his intense grip on the dice-box.

"Pray, do not let me impede you, my boy," begged Lady Christabel. "Proceed as if I were not here." When still he hesitated, she said, "If it your cast, make it now, Ralph."

There was a slight snigger from the others standing about and Ralph visibly trembled as he shook the box and, to his chagrin, threw out. Filer's smile was small and wolfish, but Lady Christabel saw it as he had intended she should. "Oh, bad luck, boy," he said in a falsely genial tone. "No matter, your fortune is bound to turn."

Lady Christabel eyed him thoughtfully. "I perceive my son has, perhaps, gone into debt to you, sir, and from your expression I gather it is not the first time. May I inquire how much he owes?"

"A mere trifle, madame. A matter of two hundred-fifty pounds. A bagatelle to folk of your standing. He could make it up in a single throw if the luck was riding with him."

"Or double it if luck is not on his side, which, I gather, is the case."

"I can deal with it, Mama," whispered the youth, but she was determined not to leave him at the mercy of these people.

"I have a terrible headache, Ralph. I fear the air in these rooms must be tainted. It cannot be good for my migraine."

Ralph rose at her implied command and Filer sneered contemptuously. "We shall settle later, then, Mawson?"

Ralph spread his hands. "I do not have the entire sum upon me at the moment, Filer, but . . ."

"But if you will send round in the late morning, sir," Lady Christabel interposed smoothly, "your demand shall be met. Two hundred-fifty, you said?"

Filer's beady little eyes seemed to snap in glee. "There is no need for haste, ma'am, if you are pressed."

"Pressed? Not at all." She snapped open her reticule. "I may even have such a sum . . . ah, no, I fear I frittered it away at faro," she laughed. "But I think you can trust that we will not flit away in the darkness, sir, over such a trifling sum."

Taking her son's arm and bestowing upon him a smile of dazzling brilliance so that all who had no mother of their own might believe that all was right in God's world.

They had not even left the Assembly Building before Ralph began to complain at her treatment of him. "Mama, how could you do such a thing? How could you shame me so before other gentlemen? I shall never hold my head up again."

"Oh, was I mistaken? Did you have the money, after all? Or have you access to it tomorrow?"

"I daresay I could get it from Jack by the day after."

"Could you? Very well, then, there is no more to be said. Send to Jack and repay me when the money arrives. But how shall you repay your brother?"

"I am not certain, Mama. I'll find a way."

Lady Christabel shook her head sadly as they walked along the now quiet pavement in the direction of their rooms. "I think, my boy, we must face up to the facts. You are not created by nature for the gambling trade. I will stand for the debt this time . . . my word, two hundred fifty pounds, Ralph . . . but in return I extract a promise."

"Anything," the youth said fervently, well aware that Jack would likely tell him to go hang.

"That I have your promise not to play again."

He was astonished. "But I cannot! All the bucks play, Mama."

"Perhaps they have fortunes of their own. When you are a 'buck' you may do as you please and go to hell in a straw basket, if you choose. But now, at this moment, you are only a foolish boy. I will pay. But if you gamble again before you reach your majority I shall take steps to disinherit you. Is that clear?"

He hung his head. "Quite clear, Mama."

"You know I am capable of it. No tricks? No sly sneaking about?"

"No tricks, Mama," Ralph agreed on a long gusty sigh.

"Good boy. You know I love you and only take these measures for your own welfare?"

"Yes, Mama dear. I know."

=16=

FROM THE DIARY of Lady Barbara Pentreath:

I do not think I flatter myself as much as Lavvy says I do. I think the Duke of Towans is strongly attracted to me, for he is always and forever looking at me in that intense and peculiar way men have of doing when they think you cannot see them. When I catch him at it he looks away quickly, but I am no fool. I would not mind being married to an older man if it meant becoming a duchess. Lavvy is forever telling me that I have no sense of proportion about the men who crowd about and that they cannot all be taken seriously. Heavens, I know that! Some have no money at all, poor things. But it is very convenient, isn't it, to have willing hands when something needs being done, whether it be to fetch a cup of fruit punch, retrieve a handkerchief or persuade Aunt to reconsider her plans. I vow I am sensible about it withal. The only one of the throng in Cheyne Spa who might hold my heart in his hand is my own Cousin R. and he is only a second son with no prospects that I know of. Mostly it is rather reassuring when older gentlemen look at one but sometimes it is rather horrid. One who arouses such a feeling in my breast is the Master of Ceremonies, a creature all prinked and painted called Beau Carlisle. He makes me shiver.

And further along the page:

> *Will not Lavvy be furious when I am a duchess and
> she still only a countess?*

It was a dreary morning and a drop in the barometer had not
improved anyone's mood. Branston had not quite removed the
breakfast things before the girls began to bicker quietly over the
services of the new maid, whom they were to share for economy's sake. Since the hiring of the staff had been left largely in
his hands he was somewhat implicated in the quarrel.

"Does she not give good service? She came with the highest
recommendations. I had thought that you Lady Lavinia . . . I
beg your pardon . . . Countess, were particularly pleased with
her."

"I sometimes wish, Branston, that you would not stand so
much on proper address. It makes me feel quite odd, since I
have known you since I was born."

"Thank you, madam, but it is as well to sort these things out
properly and become used to them. It could be embarrassing to
err in public. But about the maid, madam?"

Lavvy shrugged. "It is the old problem. Barbara feels she
deserves more attention and I daresay she does, but need it
always and forever be just when I have set the girl a task for me?
It is quite vexing to be told that Barbara instructed her to drop
what she was doing and tend to Barbara's needs at once."

"I said nothing of the kind!" protested her sister.

"As it happens, dearest, I heard you myself. It was when you
thought your hair would go out of curl with the damp."

"Oh, *that*! It only took a few minutes, not above ten. How
petty you can be, Lavvy."

"I am afraid you will have to refer to your aunt for justice. We
are not overburdened with funds just at the moment. We must
all of us make minor sacrifices until the annuity draught comes
through."

"Which it has, thank heaven," said Lady Augusta coming
through the door into the morning-room. "Not only that but a
small dividend as well. Enough for a treat, at any rate."

"I know what I shall buy," said Lady Barbara quickly. "I saw the loveliest ivory and chicken-skin fan in a window on Bow Street. I absolutely languish for it. Mayn't I have it, Aunt? Mr. Parker broke my other."

"And how, may I ask, did he manage that?"

"By being too fervent," laughed Lavinia. "He pressed Barbara's hand so hard he snapped the struts of the China-paper one you gave her. I think she really does deserve a new one, Aunt, if only as a battle compensation."

"And what will you have as a treat, my young countess?"

Lavinia shrugged. "I don't need anything that comes to mind."

Her sister would have none of it. "You see what she is like? She only does it to show me up and make me seem greedy when the truth is that she likes pretty things as much as I do."

"Is there nothing, Lavinia? I think you had better indulge yourself before your sister goes into apoplexy. Don't frown and pull a face, Barbara, or it might freeze like that and your cachet would be over."

"I *did* see some coloured cotton at the linendrapers," Lavinia conceded. "It was a very pale pink with a red dot and not too dear."

"Less than the fan, at any rate," said Lady Augusta with a trace of dry humour. "I think I saw the very one you mean when I looked for checked linen. It was not above ³/₆, as I remember."

"May we go, then, Aunt?" cried Barbara clearly quite excited at the prospect of another adornment. "If I find the fan is as pretty as I think I shall carry it to tomorrow's ball."

"Yes, yes, *do* go, in fact, for I must have a talk with Branston. But take your cloaks. The weather promises to be dirty."

The promise of bad weather was quickly kept, for it had begun to rain slightly before they left the house, but it was refreshing to be outside in the air. The maid who had been their earlier bone of contention accompanied them in an unwilling fashion, hanging back as if she might turn about and hurry home at any moment.

"Do keep up, Cora," Barbara complained. "I may want you to carry a parcel."

"Is something wrong, Cora?" asked Lavinia more kindly.

"It is me shoes, yer ladyship."

Lavinia looked at the girl's feet and saw that she was not wearing pattens but only a pair of thin-soled slippers which were already blotched with damp. "Go back to the house. Tell Branston I sent you."

"But who will carry the parcels?" Lady Barbara asked incredulously.

"How heavy will your ivory fan be?" asked the countess in return. "Run along, Cora. We must see about pattens for you."

Having procured the fan and the cotton, they turned into the bookseller's in search of diversion from the weather, but they were dejected to find that Miss Burney's *Camilla* was so popular they must put their names down if they expected to read it this season at all.

"Really, it is imperative we find something," Countess Lavinia confided to Mr. Fortes, the bookseller. "My sister requires more than needlework to divert her. She has such an active mind, you see."

Mr. Fortes scanned the shelves without bringing anything to mind, or rather the books he brought forward had already been read. Standing in the center of the shop, arms crossed at the chest and meditatively ruffling his snowy beard, he racked his brain. Then a gleam came into his eye and his fingers disentangled from the beard. "I have the very thing!"

He disappeared into a rear room and returned with a volume still redolent of the glue which had been used to finish the binding. "A book of new fairy tales, ladies!"

"Fairy tales!" Lady Barbara scoffed. "We are not children, Mr. Fortes."

"No, no, Lady Barbara, not children's tales, but fantastical stories meant to be read by adults. Most refreshing, you'll find. A splendid new talent here disclosed." If the bookseller sounded overly like one of his own advertisements it was not to be wondered at, since he himself had written them. "As well, if you purchase the volume . . . and you will never be sorry if you do, I predict . . . I daresay the author, who happens to be upon the premises at this moment, would inscribe it expressly for you, dear ladies."

Lavinia examined the book curiously. *The Kingfisher's Bride and Other Tales*, it was called. She opened it at random, read a paragraph or two, opened it again at another spot and read another. "Mr. Fortes may be right, Barbara," she said. "Come read a bit for yourself and see if you don't agree.

"You say the author is here in the shop?" she asked Fortes. "I should be most curious to meet him."

The bookseller darted out of the shop and presently returned accompanied by a pleasant looking young man. "May I present our young author, ladies," he said proudly, "Mr. Gerald Wetherbridge."

"Mr. Wetherbridge, of course!" said the countess, offering her hand. "We are already acquainted with your young author," she explained to Mr. Fortes, who smiled benignly, "though not in a literary capacity.

"You remember Mr. Wetherbridge, sister?" she asked Barbara, but, to Lady Barbara, though he seemed familiar, Gerald was merely one of the cluster of young men who seemed always at her beck and the notion that he had written a book did not unduly impress her. Something else did, however.

A harrassed-appearing man in printer's apron came bursting through the door from the shop waving a small, paper-wrapped parcel. "Thank goodness you're still here, Mr. Wetherbridge. I was afraid you had forgotten the volume of Catullus for the duke."

Gerald took it gratefully. "Thank you, John. Think of missing his birthday after all the trouble we had getting the book."

He turned back to the young women. "A new translation of Catullus, the Roman poet, you know. It was just completed by Alexander McQueen and printed in London. I think you can safely say it is fresh off the press."

Qui dono lepidum nouum libellum
arido modo pumice expolitum?

quoted Lavinia with a small smile, which Gerald answered.

"Capital! The perfect quotation, Countess."

"I wish you would let *me* in on the joke," said Barbara petulantly. "I was never tutored in Greek."

"Your sister has just spoken the opening lines, in Latin, of the book itself.

> Who shall accept my new-writ book,
> my lyrics, elegant and shy,
> all neatly dressed and polished?

"Oh, *Latin*!" sniffed Lady Barbara as if she had once spoken it well, but discarded it. "You are an acquaintance of the duke, then?" she asked with somewhat more interest.

Gerald found himself again at that quandry of identification. He settled it briefly. "I sometimes travel with him. As a sort of companion." He indicated the book. "His birthday is not for a fortnight, but I wanted to be sure to have it in good time."

"But what of your own book?" Lavinia asked.

Mr. Fortes laid a copy beside her on the counter. It was small and elegant, bound in dark blue calf and tooled in silver-gilt. "This is Mr. Wetherbridge's presentation copy for his grace, the duke."

"La, how splendid! I am quite envious!"

"Dare one enquire," asked Barbara, "how old the gentleman will be?"

Lavinia rolled her eyes heavenward. "Barbara, don't be rude."

And, really, she hadn't meant to be. "Whatever age he is, I am sure it is a very good age for a man. He is so handsome and fit that I daresay he takes very good care of himself."

"I don't think he is as old as all that," said Gerald. "Near forty, I should think, but as you say he is very fit."

"And you, Mr. Wetherbridge, will you not tell us something of your own self and interests?" asked Lady Barbara.

Gerald was beginning to wonder why he had ever thought Lady Barbara silly and shallow. Away from the thronging crowd of her admirers she seemed wonderfully simple and sincere. For the next five minutes he discoursed amiably about himself while Mr. Fortes smiled away and busied himself with stock. Lavinia, used to Barbara's tactics, spent her time perusing the shelves.

"And to think that you have written a book all by yourself," breathed Barbara. "I think that is wonderful, and very clever too. Lavinia and I must have one, of course, which I trust you will inscribe."

Gerald flushed with justifiable pride. "I hope you will allow me to make a present to you of a copy, Lady Barbara." Then added hastily, "And you, too, Countess, if you would care to have one."

He took two copies of the tales and began to write upon the flyleaf of the first. Barbara was gently caressing the smooth leather of the presentation copy. "Isn't this lovely? I vow I would give my soul for a book made just for me."

But Gerald was not so impulsive as all that, though he put the book carefully aside lest he be tempted to give it to her after all. The duke, not knowing of its existence would never miss what he had not had, but it would be poor return for all his kindness.

Their purchases selected and wrapped against the weather, the young women drifted toward the door, Gerald tagging wistfully behind. "May I not have the honour of escorting you to tea at some nearby establishment?"

"No," said the countess firmly. "I do not think that would be at all proper."

"How tiresome. Why ever not?" asked Lady Barbara.

"Because."

And that seemed to settle it until Lavinia added kindly, "But you may, if you like, walk back with us to our aunt's house."

Gerald accepted with alacrity and they stepped out of the shop to find that the rain had quite stopped, leaving in its wake a kind of hush tempered only by the click of pattens and the occasional clop of hooves. Quite peaceful for Cheyne Spa.

It was all destroyed in a moment.

Around the corner of the High Street came a curricle whose young driver obviously fancied himself a whip, for he was furiously plunging at much too great a rate for the condition of the street and the angle of the turn. From the other direction came a young man on horseback who was luckily in control of his mount, for at the sudden meeting the horses shied, the one rearing and the other, twisting in the shafts of the curricle, losing his footing. The animal turned, tipping the vehicle and throwing the driver out into the mud.

The young man suffered no apparent injury, save loss of countenance, for he quickly picked himself up, seized his crop and began to belabour the poor horse for what, after all, had been his own error of judgement. The beast, tangled as he was in the shafts and harness, could only struggle to regain his footing, rolling his eyes and screaming in panic as the driver whipped and cursed him with a will, disregarding the presence of the onlookers.

The rider of the other horse, however, was not prepared to let such negligence and abuse pass unchastised. Leaping down from his own mount he forcibly wrested the whip from the other man, as Lavinia cheered and clapped her hands in approval.

"That's enough, you young fool! Don't mistreat the horse for your own faults. And stopper up your bung. Can't you see the ladies?"

The driver, now exhibiting his condition from his stance and erratic movements as much as from the aroma of juniper which hung about him, looked about in open-mouthed surprise, swayed heavily and caught the other rider's arm for support.

"I shay . . . say . . . f'give me, ol' chap . . . bit too much of the dog's hair, doncher know?" He swept forward in a grossly exaggerated bow, which nearly upended him again and caused Gerald to run out to give the horseman a hand.

Between the two of them they quietened the horse and, unsnapping the traces while still controlling the lead, allowed him to find his footing. Then the animal was backed once more into the shafts and the traces refastened, the driver set once more in his place and, minus his whip, sent on his way. The last they saw of him he had collapsed in the seat and the horse was proceeding at its own leisurely pace, obviously possessing knowledge of the road to the stable.

Lavinia was the first to congratulate the handsome young man who had so quickly taken charge of the situation. "For," as she said later, "it was quite the most sensible way of dealing with it that could have been." When Gerald and the other man came to where the countess and Lady Barbara were waiting, she took his hand in hers and pumped it vigorously while he blushed and made self-deprecating noises. "He'd only swallowed a hare, you know. He'll sleep it off."

From along the street, clicking on their pattens, hurried two other young ladies and an older servant woman, crying out as they came, "Jack! Jack! Is that you? What are you doing here? What has happened?", never at any moment pausing for an answer, until the younger of the two, a sharp-faced but clever-looking girl, paused and stared at the countess and Lady Barbara.

"Cousin Lavinia! Cousin Barbara! Is it you?" and the young women—Elizabeth and Hermione, Lavinia and Barbara—all began to talk at once while Jack and Gerald stood by watching in amused bewilderment.

It was Elizabeth who first broke the spell of Babel amongst them, identified the cousins to their brother and brother to cousins, all the while eyeing Gerald curiously. And in a moment they had somehow fallen into pairs while walking along the street. Hermione and Barbara talking fashion, Gerald and Elizabeth comparing their impressions of the world at large and Lavinia paired with Jack, his horse on a lead, bringing up the party with talk of horses, the country, and the pleasantness of the open moors.

"I hope Aunt Augusta and your mother make up their differences," Barbara was saying wistfully to Hermione." When we saw you at the ball it was too bad for us that we could not meet."

"I didn't think you knew we were there," her cousin said frankly. "There were so many young men about you, that it would have been quite natural if you hadn't."

And Lady Barbara, sensing that she had found a devotee and crony, brushed away the diffidence. "It is no great trick, really, I'll show you how it is done, if you like."

By the time they had reached the house, all were ready for a dish of morning tea and Augusta Mabyn, having had her talk with Branston, was pleased to welcome them.

═17═

LEFT WITH BRANSTON and the final arranging of the house, Lady Augusta had bustled about like a housemaid, dusting, arranging, moving articles from one spot to another to judge the effect. All this the manservant had suffered in resigned silence . . . but making the suffering painfully obvious . . . until his mistress was obliged to mention it, if only to clear the air.

"I cannot fathom why you are so put out with me. . . . No, the wing chair in the corner, I think."

"Whatever does madam mean? . . . Should it face the window or the fire?"

"You know perfectly well what I mean. . . . Tell Cora there is a spot on the blue glass. More than one, I'll be bound! . . . You've been grumbling in the gizzard for days, my dear man. Stiff as a poker and venting your disapproval every moment."

Branston's attitude was one of a patient man gravely affronted and unjustly accused. "I am not sure that I follow madam's train of thought."

"You follow perfectly. You know exactly what I mean, just as you always do."

Branston allowed this to pass in dignified silence while Cora was summoned and the offending blue glass removed. Then he conceded, "It is only, madam, if you will forgive me . . ."

"Forgive you in advance, of course," she said tartly.

"I cannot believe, madam, that you are really going through with this plan."

"As I remember, I had your word that you would support me all the way. *We* are going through with it because there seems to me no other course. The goal is set, the money is spent, and we are about to launch. I fear it is far too late for doubts."

"But so soon, madam?"

Not for the first time Lady Augusta reflected upon the infinite nuances of Branston's tone of address to her. When an appearance of formality was required, or when, more often, he was put out with her behaviour and wished to express his disapproval, the word was sharp and precise, fairly bristling with feigned deference. When, on the other hand, he was in a relaxed, friendly or confidential state of mind, the word had quite different expression. The moods seemed to alternate this morning, running a wide gamut and disclosing, she felt, an ambivalent state of mind. This, in Branston, was so unusual that she recognised that it required her attention or she would lose her greatest support in this venture. For herself she tried on a guise of the brightest optimism.

"What luck we've had to discover a house so admirably suited to our needs, and furnished as well. We've had to do almost nothing."

"A good thing, too, madam, what with next to no staff."

"We'll find them. Don't worry so."

"Situations are two for a penny, begging your pardon. I sorely doubt you will find them for the wages we are prepared to pay."

"Then we shall have to do without."

Branston seemed nearly on the verge of tears. "Not if you expect to give your guests service of high quality. It will not do, madam, really it will not!"

Lady Augusta was tired, for she had been working as hard as he in the past few days. Her patience was also stretched to the point of exasperation. "Oh, Branston, why are you making such a do of it? You *know* I am doing what I must! If there were another way I would take it."

"Would you, madam?" he asked sadly.

"What do you mean, pray?" It was she whose tone had a chilly edge of formality now. Don't step too far, it warned. But Branston's words could be held back no longer. They came flying out as if he had been swallowing them for days. "We could have stayed in Cornwall, madam, and we should have. There were other alternatives, I am sure."

"Were there, indeed? What alternatives? To see my girls thrown away on the likes of Young Withering or the Mad Vicar? I will go penniless first! Yes, and serve, *and* sweep, *and* scrub!" She could hear that her voice was approaching hysteria and she fought to contain it.

But the manservant was as exhausted as she and he chose to misinterpret what she was saying. "Both of the gentlemen are worthy men, I don't doubt, madam." It was not a statement but a retort, and he carried it even further. "I believe even you entertained the notion of their worthiness at one time."

There was an endless moment of shocked silence between them. Hers at what he had said, his that he had had the temerity to say it. Each turned away from the other. A long standing relationship swung perilously in the balance.

She bridged the chasm gracefully, pretending the impertinence had not been uttered.

"*You* are a man of great worth, come to that."

And he leapt to her rescue by taking her lead. "I have no matrimonial ambitions, if you please, madam," he said smoothly, in a tone light as thistledown. "I would not presume to the state of Malvolio."

Now she could smile. "No cross-gartering for you, eh?" It was a strained and limping reply, but it served until Cora returned with the blue glass, now polished and gleaming.

"Have the young ladies returned yet, Cora?" Lady Augusta asked.

"No, ma'am, not yet. I hope I didn't do wrong, going off from them like that?"

"Not at all. I should have seen that you were not properly shod. I daresay the two of them will not entirely outrage propriety before they return."

When Cora had gone out again, her ladyship observed, "A pity we cannot find more like that one."

Branston agreed. "We were lucky there, madam, by any

measure." They worked in silence until he ventured to ask, "On what occasion do you expect to open the house to guests, madam?"

"I don't follow you."

His brow furrowed thoughtfully. "I do not think you can exactly cry, *look! look!* can you now? You daren't open with a splash."

"I suppose not. I shall have to ease into it slowly to let the town become accustomed to the thought of a lady running an establishment. It will be quite shocking to some, though the Londoners will be familiar enough with the notion, thanks to Lady Cheseborough."

The clamour of the doorknocker put an end to the discussion. Branston put aside his apron and went to open it. The crowd of young people seemed to pour in with the young countess and Lady Barbara in high spirits at being among their peers.

They are only children, after all, thought their aunt. I sometimes forget that.

"See whom we've found, Aunt Augusta!"

"I *can* see. Hermione, how you've grown! And Eliza, welcome!" She looked inquiringly at the two young men. "Mr. Wetherbridge I recognize as well, but . . ."

"It is Jack, Aunt Augusta, my eldest brother!" cried Elizabeth. "Come up from the country to be brave and gallant."

Nothing would do but that the whole excursion be recounted, the tale of Cousin Jack's heroism, and even of Mr. Wetherbridge's new volume of tales. "Do show it her, Mr. Wetherbridge. She of all people will appreciate it," said Lavinia. "My aunt is very well educated."

"You make me sound a bluestocking," Lady Augusta protested.

Gerald was vainly fumbling with the string of one of the parcels, but Barbara impatiently corrected him. "No, not that one. That is your birthday gift for the duke."

The eyes of Branston and his mistress met across the heads of the others. The occasion seemed to have been found.

* * *

The duke, himself, was in rather a disconsolate mood as he was admitted to the salon of Mrs. Fitzherbert's house. The lady was already seated by the window as if she had been expecting him and had been keeping watch. She extended her hand without rising and, as he bent over it, he said, "I am sorry, madam, I seem to have failed you."

The lady shook her head. "Not necessarily. You kept your appointment?"

"I kept it but he did not. I was met by the equerry and frozen out with 'His Royal Highness begs to be excused', spoken in that demmed upper class nasal tone that makes you want to ball up your fists and begin a mill."

"How funny you are. You outrank the equerry by several degrees, I expect."

"Ah, but he embodies in himself his royal master. But you do not seem surprised. Did you expect me to be turned away when you sent me?"

"Not when I asked you to represent me," said Mrs. Fitzherbert. "I had reason later to believe you might be shut out."

Towans smiled in spite of himself. "The Fitzherbert secret service again? Your maid, I take it, had infiltrated the Grand Hotel."

"No," said Mrs. Fitzherbert, "I guessed it because His Royal Highness was here."

"Here? In this house?" The duke slapped his thigh. "By Gad, the man has no shame."

"Not only in this house, but in this room and sitting in the chair you occupy, I believe."

"And you?"

"Oh, I did not see him at all," she replied airily. "I played the coward and huddled away in the boudoir the while he alternately commanded, pleaded, and wept loudly enough to be heard through the panelling. He made sure of that. It was quite a display. When I returned he was still performing."

"When you returned? You were in the boudoir?"

"Ah, but the boudoir has two doors, as of course does this house. I merely went out for a bit of shopping. When I came back he was just winding down. He sounded quite hoarse, poor thing. I believe he is not adequately trained in public histrionics. I wonder if Talma might be lured back to England."

The duke laughed shortly. "I doubt that the leading actor of the *Comédie Française* would come back to give the Prince of Wales a set of elocution lessons."

"I don't know," she said. "He was, after all, raised in England. He must have some affection for us."

"Not that I'm aware of. I believe he is a great admirer of General Bonaparte."

"Alas!" she said with a mock sigh. "He is lost to us forever. Poor George must go untutored."

The duke found himself indulgently beginning to relax in the sunny warmth of Mrs. Fitzherbert's charm. He knew, this morning, what drew Prince George back to her again and again.

"What, exactly, do you propose to do, madam? I daresay the question of your status and future may be arranged by your advocates in London as much as by me?"

Mrs. Fitzherbert was at once contrite. "Oh, my dear friend, did you think I was drawing you into this tangled net for all time? I asked only that you perform that little errand this morning. Since it has failed I ask no more of you."

The duke held up a cautionary finger. "Pray, do not so quickly put me out to the dustman. I may have a trick or two to your advantage, after all."

= 18 =

IN THE TWO weeks since the revolutionary ball at which the Prince first appeared the atmosphere had completely changed. Consequently, the next one promised to be a terrible crush. The celebrity of the King's son and that of the Duke of Towans, combined with the hint of the possible presence of the notorious Mrs. Fitzherbert guaranteed that every ambulatory soul in Cheyne Spa would make an appearance. Every belle, every beau, every queen of society and every hanger-on to the fringe of it were packing themselves into the Upper Rooms, staring hungrily into each other's faces as if about to ask, "Should I know you? Are you anybody? Will I waste my time in talking to you or will I compromise myself if I am seen with you?" As a result few people talked to anyone at all, or merely to those with whom they had come. Others wandered about with a feverish and preoccupied air as if they knew everyone but had no time to talk. They impressed no one, for no one cared. They were interested in Persons of Importance, hard to come by since Cheyne Spa was of secondary rank. Only those three interested them: the duke who regularly appeared, the Prince who had twice shown himself, and the Prince's cast-off, whom he now wished to put-on again, had never appeared at all.

But the Duchess of Doddington was there, having been taught the rudiments of the waltz by her majordomo. The Mayor, Mr. Tobias, was there, of some celebrity himself but as eager as any to be titillated by social distinction. And Filer, of course, was there, slinking about on the edges of the crowd like a wild dog waiting to snap up any stragglers. And certainly most

125

of *our* acquaintance were there, each for reasons of their own. Well, no, not everyone, since the Prince who had, all this time, been shunned by Mrs. Fitz, disappointed all by declining to parade his chagrin. But Gerald was there, hoping he had an inside track with Lady Barbara. The countess and her cousin, Jack, were present, in separate parties, each bearing the hope of seeing the other, and also there were Jack's mother, sisters, and brother Ralph. Filer had his eye on Ralph.

No one was any more interested in the minuet, not even the old duchess. It was all the waltz, the waltz, the waltz. Singular that a dance derived ultimately from the German peasants' *ländler* should be the craze in a proper English spa, but perhaps not. The Hanovers were German, after all. And besides which, there was something smooth and sensuous in it. One could lose oneself in the rhythm without seeming a fool to onlookers, a decided advantage in Albion.

Lady Augusta and the duke, having overseen their duties, one way or the other, were, with a few hardy souls, walking along the colonnades of the rotunda above the Upper Rooms and engaging in a conversation which, as all their recent conversations seemed to do, verged on the recognisably personal. Lady Augusta had only just disclosed her plans.

"What? A gambling house? Madam, surely you jest? No lady of . . ."

"Oh, fiddle, Towans! In London it is done all the time. I could name five 'ladies of quality', fallen on slim times, who have resorted to such measures—derived the major part of their income from it, in fact—and the world has not tumbled about them. No one minded unless it be some staid old fish like my cousin Christabel. I daresay she will raise a hue and cry, but somehow I am prepared to give up the advantage of Christabel's society."

The duke had to laugh at this. "I think you should look in the Lower Rooms some late evening if you believe your cousin does not take a flyer now and then. Her play is steep."

"I don't doubt it, but it would not prevent her from dinning me." She became pensive, then brightened. "I wouldn't need the income if I could marry off the gels without it." She looked up at him archly. "Into the peerage, preferably."

They walked a few steps in silence, the duke unable to tell if she were joking or serious. Deciding that her speech was made somewhere between the two, he considered how he should respond to it. He cleared his throat and then said firmly, "I am perhaps being premature, madam, but I must say to you that there is no possible hope of my asking for the hand of either of your wards in marriage. I have intimated as much in the past."

The Lady Augusta must perforce take such a bald statement in stride, and she did, but not without a parting salvo. "Barbara is *very* fond of you, sir, and I must remind you that the blood of my wards is as noble as your own."

"Better, I have no doubt, since *my* dukedom is of fairly recent date and granted for no very creditable reason," he answered mildly. "But, there it is."

Lady Augusta considered this. "I cannot suppose it is because of dowry, though, I admit, we have been less than candid in that quarter." She sighed meaningfully. "I was never very good at dissimulation. I daresay if I had been, my present state might be considerably improved. Not to mention that of the girls."

"You seem to care for them greatly."

"As if they were my own daughters. I am afraid I do not serve them well."

"Are you not curious enough to ask why, though I did consider her, I have decided not to speak for the young countess?"

"Lavvy? I thought . . . but, Barbara . . ."

"There was never any question of Lady Barbara. It was . . . it is . . . the intelligence and simplicity of the countess which I find attractive. Lady Barbara would be the early death of a husband who could not offer an equal vitality of youth. No, it was Countess Lavinia I thought of until I realised that her charm, while great, had its source . . . its inspiration, perhaps . . . in another place."

Lady Augusta bristled, thinking it a slur upon her ward. "Does it, indeed?"

"Yes, dear madam, I think it does." He looked rather oddly at her, a mixture of affection and annoyance. "What an exasperating conversation this is."

She was determined to be prickly. "I hadn't realised that, but since you find it so you are at liberty to terminate it, your grace. I have no desire to keep you from your other concerns."

He frowned. "What do you mean by that, pray?"

And once begun she could not stop, even though it should not be her concern. "I have heard, sir, that you spend a certain amount of time going in the back door of a certain house while the Prince waits in the front."

He had the superbity to laugh in her face! "In truth, Lady Augusta, you have imperfect spies."

They paused, looking out over the town. There was no moon, but the sky was black velvet and diamonds. "In fact, I *am* about my business, you know. Have you any notion of the point I make?"

"How should I, sir? So far you have told me that neither of my wards is up to standard, nor, it seems, is a certain lady. I wonder who, then, is?"

"You are, Augusta, as you would know if you would take the time to listen."

"What?" For once the Lady Augusta was, as they say, knocked off her perch.

"Have you had no idea that it was because of you that I have no interest in your nieces?"

"But I have been for many years a . . . widow . . . almost a spinster."

"Stupid word. Were you confined to the corner of your brother's house with spinning wheel at hand? I know that you are a widow and for how many years. I know that your marriage was short but happy, unlike my own. I recognise that you were devoted to your brother, for all his faults, and are now so to his children. But I do not think it a service to *them* to let them be a barrier to your own happiness."

"And you believe you can assure that?"

"I think I could do very well at trying. We are of similar views, and temperaments singular to our generation. Are you aware, my dear . . . do you remember? . . . that we are of an age within six months and you the junior? There are things I do not fathom. Why is it that a man in his prime at forty is a catch, but a woman of thirty-nine and six months is doomed to lead apes in hell? Is there a law about that? Is it somewhere incised in stone?"

Lady Augusta tried to laugh, but found she had not enough breath. Why was she trembling? Shakily, she asked, "What is it, exactly, that you are saying, Towans?"

His voice both softened in tone and roughened in timbre. "What I am saying, dearest Augusta, is that in the few short days that we have seen each other again, I have realised what a consummate fool I was to have allowed you out of my life for so long."

"You surely cannot be . . ."

"And I am further saying, my dear, that the idea of another span of years without you somewhere very near is unthinkable."

Lady Augusta could never say why she laughed just at that moment. It, conceivably, changed the course of the conversation.

"Good Lord, are you proposing to me, Towans?"

The duke looked at her for a long moment, and then a small smile curled about his handsome lips. Not at all uncomfortable in his reply, he said, "No, madam, I am not . . . or not exactly. Let us call this a strictly honourable pre-proposal speech. I believe we have mutually missed a great deal by not knowing each other in all this time. Naturally, we have changed and matured over those years. I propose . . . pre-propose, perhaps . . . that we reacquaint ourselves with a view toward a closer relationship in the future."

"One that is strictly honourable?"

"Strictly."

"Strictly. Would you have it otherwise?"

"Oh, la! What a disappointment you men are! Could you not have allowed me the spice of believing myself secretly notorious?" She paused and clapped fingers to her lips. "Oh, lud!"

"What is it?"

"I just thought of Barbara. What on earth will she say of this? I know she had her mind firmly set on acquiring you."

"I notice you do not say love. I am glad of that. When I go up to London tomorrow I shall make enquiries as to how young women are making their comeouts these days. It is still my obligation to help in any way I can, regardless of what we decide of our future history."

"What shall you be doing in London?" Even as she said the words Lady Augusta recognised how proprietary they sounded. "Forgive me, I . . ."

"Not at all. I have no secrets from you. It is a diplomatic errand to the court on behalf of a certain lady."

"Ah, and if I speculated on her identity?"

"You would doubtless be correct."

They descended the stair into the Upper Rooms and took up their social burdens. The duke was at once beseiged by anxious mamas and Lady Augusta by courtly young men who wished, for the most part, introductions to her wards. She looked carefully about to see if she could even discover those young females, and spied them easily enough by the clusters of young men who were either engaged in courting them, or watching enviously those who did.

Lady Augusta saw that young Jack Mawson appeared to have the edge where the countess was concerned. It pleased Augusta well enough, but she wondered how Christabel would feel about it. Certainly the idea of a country life for Lavinia was ideal, but was Jack, Christabel's son, the ideal husband?

As for Barbara, one could hardly say to whom she was giving her attention. Certainly it was not undivided. It was easy, though, to see that she had noticed the return of her aunt and the duke from the rotunda colonnade, for when she and Lady Augusta caught each other's eyes, there was more than a suggestion of irritation present in her expression. Wryly Lady Augusta wondered what was to come from that direction. She could hardly *say* much, since nothing had ever been stated aloud, but the undercurrent would be there. Pray God it would not carry away the affection between aunt and niece.

There was a buzz of sudden conversation and then a slow cessation of any talking at all. Instead there was a kind of hush as if every person in the rooms were afraid to speak for fear something might be missed.

"What is it?" whispered someone near Lady Augusta. She turned and saw that Lady Christabel Mawson was standing beside her. "What is happening?"

Lady Augusta shook her head and shrugged without speaking.

And then they both saw, for the crowd parted as readily as the sea waves of Egypt, cloven, as it were, by a force greater than themselves. And through the open pathway came a lady of their own age, unescorted and unwelcomed by any of them. And now across the crowd came the whisper upon whisper of "Fitz . . . Fitz . . . Fitzherbert . . ."

"Good heavens," said Lady Christabel. "It *is* she."

Lady Augusta looked about for Towans, but saw him nowhere.

"Can you imagine the gall of it?" whispered her cousin into her ear. "That woman . . . coming here!"

And presumably her sentiment was shared, for every expression seemed closed and forbidding; except, of course, for those simpletons who merely stood goggle-eyed and slack-mouthed in shock.

There was something in the face of the Prince's wife that touched Lady Augusta deeply. It had taken courage of a high degree to brave the opinion of this hostile crowd, to whom she was not a wronged wife but a woman of notoriety. There was pride in that face but there was discomfiture as well, as if she were expecting someone who had not yet appeared.

Augusta had no doubt it was Towans, and the duke was not to

be seen. Lady Augusta Mabyn stepped forward and swept into a generous curtsey. "Good evening, Mrs. Fitzherbert. Such a pleasure to see you here."

She was twice rewarded for her gesture. First, the warm smile of gratitude from Mrs. Fitzherbert; secondly, that she could almost *feel* rather than hear the hiss of outraged indignation which issued from her cousin Christabel's lips.

19

CARLTON HOUSE BELONGED to the Prince, there was no doubt of that. The Princess of Wales only lived there. Lived in splendour, it is true, but unhappily. Considering the state of affairs between husband and wife, it is perhaps as well that the residence was so large that they could spend their lives without meeting. He had his associates, his mistresses and his friends . . . though, thank heaven the odious Lady Jersey, whom he had foisted on his wife as a lady-in-waiting, was gone. She had her own associates, though fewer. In a moment of rare generosity the Prince had stated that he had no objections to her entertaining as he did except that supper parties ought not to include any gentlemen save the husbands of her ladies. And this was all very well, except that no one called. Everyone took care to be on the good side of the man who would one day be their king.

Sometimes she did not even know when he was in residence.

> For particular reasons, said The Times, the Prince was not present at the King's birthday celebrations and has set out, incognito, for Wessex. The Princess of Wales remains at court.

"See this, Arbuthnot?" cried Caroline. "You see? He goes to his mistress and the whole world knows!"

But her dresser, Mrs. Arbuthnot, was too wise to respond. She knew, as all the world knew, of Mrs. Fitzherbert and she had heard, as all the court had heard, of his illegal marriage to her. She had no intention of becoming embroiled in such a discussion with her employer.

"My papa had a mistress, you know," Caroline observed. "I suppose all men do."

"Perhaps Your Highness should not speak of such things."

But Caroline was not to be deterred. "Ach, she was a marvel, that one. The very beautifullest and cleverest creature imaginable. I learned more from that woman than from any other in my life."

"Really, ma'am!" But Mrs. Arbuthnot could not resist the temptation. "How would Your Highness know such a woman?"

"Why should I not? Why, her apartments were only along the corridor from my own."

Mrs. Arbuthnot was aghast. "Do you mean to say that your father's mistress actually lived in the ducal palace, ma'am?"

"How not? He dined in state with her once a week, ain't? How inconvenient to go out. And think of the expense of maintaining an extra household! My papa is a very careful man."

Mrs. Arbuthnot knew that no good could come of the familiarity on which the Princess insisted between herself and her servants, but, really, it was such an education, wasn't it?

"But what did the good duchess, your mother, say? Was she not outraged?"

The Princess Caroline chuckled deep in her throat, as if this absurdity was beyond consideration. "Mama? Mama was never outraged, poor thing. She had not the courage. And how outraged over amiable Mlle. Hertzfeldt? No, they were the best of friends and often managed Papa between them for his own good. Especially if a new rival was in the offing.

"Better the evil known than the unknown evil, not?"

Even Arbuthnot had to laugh at that. Certainly the Princess was odd with her peculiar German ways, but there was not a cruel bone in her body. Coarse and overblown she might be, as many said, but her heart was warm.

Even Caroline knew that her tongue often ran away with her and that it was her greatest failing. Too often she said things only to startle or to startle others into amusement. Or when she herself was wounded.

Which was often.

Sometimes she felt that all of her life since she arrived in England had been one long battle. In Brunswick they had told her of this Gentleman Prince, and his minister Malmesbury fetched his portrait and the offer of his hand in marriage. Well, why not? Mama was English, after all. They could not be so terrible.

So she had accepted the portrait of the handsome young man and worn it on a ribbon around her neck like a decoration of honour upon her breast. People smiled at her and congratulated her and intimated how lucky she was. At twenty-six, after all, it is something to find such a husband.

And then she had met him and what did the Prince do? What did he say, this First Gentleman in Europe? Caroline tried to kneel, but George took one look at her and said—incredibly— as he broke sharply away and strode across the room, "Malmesbury, I am not well; pray get me a glass of brandy."

Caroline neither showed how crushed she was nor crumbled, only observed, when the Prince had swept out of the room, "*Mon dieu*! Is the Prince always like that? I find him very fat, and nothing as handsome as his portrait." It was spiteful satisfaction.

Even Malmesbury had no answer.

The wheels had been set in motion. They would be married in three days' time. There was nothing to do but smile.

And smile. And lie to Mama and Papa about how happy you were.

And smile.

And Lady Jersey was always there.

But enough of that. Lady Jersey was there no longer though she had taken a house almost next door. And *The Times* had something to say about that as well, deploring it in a simpering way.

Gott, but she had tried! And everything she did was wrong. Now she understood that she had listened and taken advice from the wrong people. If she had enlisted his sympathy, perhaps, he would have turned protective, but she must show him how she did not care and that he could not hurt her. They all said how generous he was, but it was never shown to her.

For a brief while, during the time she was pregnant, she was someone of importance. It was almost a miracle that she had achieved that state for the Prince had been so drunk on brandy on their wedding night that he had fallen insensible into the fireplace where she left him and he remained all night.

So much for the First Gentleman in Europe.

In the morning he had recovered only enough to climb into her bed. And exactly nine months (less only three days, *The Times* duly noted) the Princess Charlotte was born.

Nothing became better. Now they had the child over which to quarrel, she supposed, and it had come to this, that he could be gone to Wessex for a fortnight before she even knew that he was not living in the house.

Arbuthnot came back into the room with a sealed paper in her hand, heavy paper with the embossment of a noble, though recent, house.

Curiously the King's daughter-in-law broke the seal and read the contents aloud.

> *The Duke of Towans would be greatly honoured if Her Royal Highness, the Princess of Wales, would grant him the favour of a personal audience on a private matter.*

Mon dieu! And they said the duke was a very handsome man. What could it be that brought him to her? And what could be the private matter of which he spoke?

= 20 =

"ABOUT HOW MANY persons have you invited to be your guests, Aunt?" asked the Countess Lavinia. She was dressed in a light morning frock of pale yellow muslin and her aunt found it both attractive and fashionable, an area of things to which the countess had, in the past, paid less than proper attention. It was amazing how a gel would alter her viewpoint when there was a man in the picture.

She and her ward were still in the breakfast room because it was the only chamber of the large house which took the morning light, and for a long time each day, facing, as it did rather to the southeast. They had decorated it with pale colours, as well—ivory and muted greens. Just above the picture rail was painted a Greek key design in a darker viridian which harmonised well with the Hepplewhite furnishings. Since Lady Augusta anticipated that evening illumination would be of most importance to her future plans the comparative darkness of the remainder of the house made little difference. It had, in fact, driven down the terms of the lease a trifle, but the breakfast room remained the favourite gathering place of the household.

"About fifty, I should think. I have rather lost count. Where do we stand, Branston?"

The manservant, hovering about in the hope of being included in the discussion, concurred. "About that, I think, milady, though not all the invitations have had replies."

"There will always be some who will not accept, of course," said Lady Augusta.

"I beg your pardon, madam," Branston said decisively. "I am

sure *everyone* will accept and fight for the privilege. I think you should expect that."

"Mercy, do you think so?"

"It is in the duke's honour, ma'am. Would *you* let anything interfere, ma'am, if you had been invited?"

"I am giving the party, Branston. I shall naturally attend."

"I think you misunderstand him, Aunt," the countess interposed. "I believe that he means if you were a scheming social climber you would give your soul to attend a party given in honour of the Duke of Towans, would you not?"

The lady laughed. "La, Lavinia, what do you think I am if *not* a scheming social climber, as you so aptly put it? Why do you suppose I am *giving* the party, if not to climb? It is the perfect way to introduce the gaming salon."

With the right of a long-term retainer, Branston asked a pertinent question. "Do you think, madam, that it is exactly the right thing to do?"

Lady Augusta shrugged her lovely shoulders, which the French had, years ago in Paris, called *des épaules impertinentes.* "Can you think of a more splendid way?"

"But on the duke's birthday, Aunt," asked Lavinia doubtfully. "Are you certain he will have no objections?"

"Pooh! What objections could he have? I am not setting up a shop, after all."

"Mightn't he resent it, milady?" the manservant asked carefully. "Might he not feel he was being . . ." he paused for the right word ". . . being exploited?"

"How absurd! Branston, the duke and I are old friends. He knows I would never embarrass him in any way."

"I hope you are right, ma'am?"

Why was she feeling so defensive about this? "In any case there will be no serious gaming on that night, only a little diversion among intimates."

"Intimates, Aunt?" crowed Countess Lavinia. "Fifty intimates in a short time in a strange town? You have done well, I must say."

"Please don't be dreary, Lavvy, you know exactly what I

mean. The tables will be there merely for the convenience of those who are not musical, and as a sort of introduction. Eventually, I trust, this house will be seen as a pleasant alternative to the rather grimly serious atmosphere of the Lower Rooms. Gaming here, I hope, will be seen as a pleasure, not an obsession."

"So that folk may lose their money in a social setting, madam?" asked the servant slyly, for which he received a sharp look.

"Branston, are you being forward?"

"Certainly not, madam," with a straight face. "I am sorry if you think so."

"I would appreciate a shade less irony in your tone, if you please. Does the silver not need polishing?"

"I will attend to it, madam," he said and exchanged an understanding look with the countess as he went out of the room.

"How heavenly that Faltinelli is still in Cheyne and has agreed to sing that night. The duke is very appreciative of him and I hope that he will be more in his customary voice and that you and Barbara will come to see what a great artist he is. As well as a charming person."

"Has Mrs. Fitzherbert answered your invitation, Aunt? Do you think she will come to the celebration?"

"No, I have heard nothing from her as yet, but I suspect she may attend if only to spite the Prince. She was so delighted to have scored off him by eluding him and attending the ball, that I think she will not pass a second opportunity."

"But she will see the Prince here, will she not?" asked Lavinia.

"No," said Lady Augusta, "for I have not invited him."

A voice echoed from the adjoining room. "You have neglected to invite the Prince of Wales, madam?"

"I have never heard you in the incredulous mode, Branston. It is quite a novelty. For once I seem to have stopped you completely. No, since this is a private affair, not a public function, I saw no obligation to include His Royal Highness, particularly since he is not a favourite of the duke, nor the duke of him. Pray, do not look so alarmed. It is not *lese majesté* to exclude a prince from a supper party."

"After inviting fifty others, madam?"

"Fifty or five, it boots nothing. It is my house and the choice is mine entirely. It cannot reflect on the duke, for the decision has come from me, and if the Prince comes *she* will not, and I rather liked her."

Lavinia's smile seemed almost a reflexion of the morning light. "I believe you must have won her heart forever, Aunt, with your courage at the ball. I think it was a marvelous gesture to welcome her like that when every one else was turning a very cold shoulder."

Lady Augusta's face grew rather serious. "It was no gesture, child. I did it for two reasons. One, because I know she is an old and dear friend of the duke, and the duke is an old and dear friend of mine. And two, because I saw the look in her eyes and I knew how I would feel in the same position; sent to Coventry by a gaggle of ninnyhammers for no better reason than refusing to surrender her virtue before taking marriage vows. The fault is all on the side of the government, I do assure you, and Prince or not, laws or not, that man is no more than a bigamist, and my heart goes out to the two wretched women he has drawn into this."

Countess Lavinia was clever enough to be worried.

"I hope you will not repeat such things outside this house, Aunt Augusta."

"Even I am not such a temeritous fool as that, my dear." She peered closely into the face of the countess. "You seem unusually bright today, by the way, Lavinia. Has something transpired that I know nothing of and should?"

"Why, no, Aunt."

"Do not pull that demure face with me, my girl. If it has not yet happened, you anticipate that it will shortly?"

"Perhaps," said her ward. "It is too early to tell."

"I can only say I do not envy you the thought of having

Christabel Mawson for a mother-in-law. I should think you will go mad."

"Oh, Aunt Christabel is not so terrible. I rather like her. I know she is all spines on the exterior, like a hedgehog, but underneath she is often quite tender."

"Also like a hedgehog, I believe. Or so the gypsies say."

"The gypsies?" cried Lavinia incredulously. "You have never said you knew anything about gypsies! What is this about hedgehogs, then?"

"I believe they roll them in mud and bake them in a campfire. When the dried, baked mud is knocked away the spines and the hide come with it, I understand. I can assure you that the flesh *is* sweet and tender."

"How extraordinary you are. Fancy knowing such a thing. Did you learn that on your travels?"

"Among other things. We did not live only in Paris, you understand."

Lavinia sighed. "When I was a child I wanted to run away with a gypsy caravan that used to camp in our lower field. Do you remember?" Her eyes took on a faraway look.

"Aunt?" she asked.

"Yes, dear?"

"Were you very happy?"

"When I was married? Yes. Very happy."

"Do you think I shall be?"

"If you choose to be, my pet. Liking Christabel is a good beginning, and I should think Jack offers you a good chance at it. But the decision to be happy or discontented usually rests with ourselves, don't you think?"

At that moment Lady Barbara's voice, strident with annoyance, came cutting through the quiet atmosphere of the house. "Really, Cora, when will you learn that a lady must never be kept waiting at the door?"

— 21 —

YOUNG WITHERING WAS terrified, although he would never dream of admitting it. They had been careening along at full career since leaving Penwith and he was heartily sick of it, of the acute discomfort of the high-perch seat and with the Mad Vicar's endless and repetitive monologues about racing, about hunting, and about his prospects of marrying the Countess Lavinia. He appeared quite sanguine of success in that quarter and built higher upon it with every mile.

"The title cannot come to me, of course, but it will to my son. Superfluous in any case, don't y'know. I am, after all, the Vicar of old St. Clarus and that is something in itself, eh? Fine old church, what? Fine old living, come to that. Never lose it, you know, the gift of it being with the Pentreath family."

"I say, Falsworth!" Withering could feel his words on the wind.

"Yes, old chap?"

"Isn't this a bit dangerous?"

"Marrying upward? Nonsense. Done all the time. How do you think these old houses continue, eh? Do it by marrying for new blood, you see. Fresh strain and all that. Just as with horses, don't yer know!"

"No, no! This abominable speed, I mean. Must we travel like madmen?"

"Only way, my friend, the only way. Do you want the season to be over before we arrive?"

"I only hope our lives will not be over before we arrive!"

Withering thought disconsolately of his staid, chaise and

careful driver, vastly regretting his capitulation to Falsworth's insistant invitation to accompany him to Cheyne Spa.

"To see what the ladies are up to, you know."

And it had seemed like an excellent idea at the time for, though he believed that Lady Barbara had been convinced of his own worthy qualities and the substantial value of his assets, still she *was* a young girl and young girls are of changeable minds. To give the man his due, the thought that he might be making a fool of himself *did* cross his mind, but the alliance of older men and younger women was not unheard of, after all, and had a long relatively honourable history. But such reflexions were futile while his brain was being jogged in this intolerable fashion.

He allowed himself to lapse into a numbed silence, merely nodding like an automaton from time to time to give the illusion of following the conversation. Already his hat had been twice lost and his patience a dozen times over, as much with himself as with the vicar and his racing vehicle. What a fool he had proved himself to be!

On through Teighton and Tamar's Well, Barsley and St. Severn. Bone weary, mouths dry and caked with dust, they came to rest at Elspeth Bridge.

"Bedroom and breakfast, gentlemen? Yes, sir! Just step that way, sir! Gentlemen's valises and hot water to the front chamber, boy!" (The *boy* had passed sixty.) "You will find a sea-coal fire laid, gentlemen. Gets dampish hereabouts at night, y'know. All a part of the service. We aims to make our custom feel at home with us, gentlemen." And they were whisked away. "Front chamber! Front chamber!"

Pity poor Withering. Now Falsworth's words were no longer blown away by the wind and he seemed to be reiterating much the same series of sentiments with which he had whiled away the day's drive. Falsworth, in fact, seemed much content with a very small supply of sentiments which he used over and over in various combinations. No bad thing in a vicar, perhaps, who must drive home the tenets of doctrine, but death in a travelling companion. He appeared prepared to offer them up again, still again, until Withering pleaded exhaustion and begged to be excused.

"You're not a travelling-man, lawyer! Not a fellow of the road, what? Not used to it! I dessay you'd get accustomed to it quick enough given the opportunity. Nothing like the road and a fine pair at a fast clip, eh? Springing along! Nothing to beat it, nothing, what?"

Alas, tired as he was, Young Withering did not rest at all. Instead he tossed and turned, too exhausted to let himself sink into sweet oblivion, even given the excellent beds in the front chamber of The Parson's Trotter at Elspeth Bridge.

In the morning, when the abominable cheeriness of the vicar smote him like a fiery sword, he groaned woefully, but reflected that they would be in Cheyne Spa in time for tea. With any luck he would locate Lady Augusta and her household almost immediately, lay his case before her, and have Lady Barbara's answer before the week was out.

The Reverend Falsworth did not even consider such things. To him all this had been, not a mere excuse for stretching the horses, but certainly a reason, and a chance to escape the tedium of St. Clarus for a bit. He had no doubt of the outcome of his suit with the countess. She was a sensible, good-hearted country girl and would understand the advantages of such a match and the shared interests which would make it even more attractive. He sang as they flew along the roads, mostly an old hunting song of red coats and baying hounds and the thrill of the moment when the quarry makes its stand against the hunters. Rum and stirring stuff, that!

What, ho! The song of the road! Nothing like it. Even with such a stick as Withering for a companion. He wondered if the lawyer was aware that he had snored most of the night? Not much chance of a happy marriage there, for he couldn't imagine that Lady Barbara would put up with such behaviour. It was all in the mind, of course. Didn't have to snore if you set your mind to it.

On through market towns like Balstrop and villages like Paul's Pride (a corruption of *False* Pride, it was generally acknowledged) and Autreleigh (generally pronounced Adderly), and that place once called Castra Parvulorum but now, even in guidebooks, called Fardles.

Daresay there is some semantic law at work there, he thought, diminution of language or some such thing. He had probably had it at school, but, Lord, he was no scholar, and that was, it seemed, a century ago.

Beside him, Withering slumbered on the sly. Wonderful how the chap kept his balance like that. Did it all day yesterday, too.

=== 22 ===

IN THE HOUSE in Hawk's Lane all was not well. For one thing Lady Christabel had found herself in a rather embarrassing position for a lady. The thrills of faro had been her undoing. The challenge of setting herself up against the odds, against the gods of fortune, as it were, had been her downfall. The play had become more grand and the sense of power more intoxicating and then, quite suddenly it seemed, she had no more money and she stood in the dreadful position of being indebted to Beau Carlisle, of all people, the *doyen* of the spa. If she did not find a way to pay she would be ruined socially. Not that *these* people in Cheyne Spa meant anything, really, but she had always felt so much above them, so superior to their petty impulses and crazes. It was, really, quite unsettling.

She could have gone to Jack, of course, and Jack was here to be gone to, but there was this business of Augusta's girl and she wasn't sure she was altogether happy about such a turn of events. Not but what the girl seemed pliable enough and might be trained into a good mistress of Fogg's Hall, but there was the danger of closer association with Augusta, and that had always meant trouble, hadn't it? They had never agreed since they were girls.

She dressed and prepared to go out, summoning one of the maids to attend her. She wore a silk turban in two colours, gold and lemon, and carried her tilting-parasol against the sun. The lace shawl was for respectability. Not everyone could still have lace of this quality. It said something about who you were.

The maid walked a respectful three steps behind her and it

146

was almost as if Lady Christabel had the advantage of solitude. It left her mind free to consider her problems. She wouldn't be at all surprised if Augusta had not engineered this situation with Jack and Lavinia. Everyone knew the three of them—four if you counted that dreadful manservant—had come to Cheyne to find husbands for the girls.

She had never cared for Branston. She could not bear servants who used irony as a weapon against their superiors. Though there was a case for asserting that it was Branston alone who had held the household together since the fire. Beautiful Pentreath. Such a loss. Probably due to the carelessness of servants. Allow that sort of irony and they became familiar, become familiar and they became careless. Poor Pentreath. Such a beautiful house.

The gentleman who was approaching her looked rather familiar but she could not attach a name to the face for a moment, and then it came to her. His name was Filer, she recalled. A man dear Ralph had gambled with before he gave it up at her insistance. A nice enough type, she supposed, but she had been very careful to pay Ralph's debt in full from her first phenomenal winnings at Carlisle's faro table, and the man had never bothered either of them again. He had always smiled and lifted his hat when he had seen her. London, obviously. Country gentlemen did not have such manners.

"Good afternoon, Lady Christabel. A lovely day, is it not?"

"A lovely day, Mr. Filer. So nice to have seen you again."

"Your lovely daughters are well, I hope?"

She assented comfortably. "But you seem troubled, Mr. Filer. Is something amiss?"

He hesitated, appearing distinctly uncomfortable it seemed to her. Then it struck her. Did he wish to convey something to *her*? . . . My Lord, was it Ralph? . . . She must be brave.

"If there is something you must communicate to me, sir, perhaps it is better said without listeners?" Filer looked distinctly relieved. She motioned the maid away a little, afraid of what the girl might overhear.

"May I give you a dish of tea, madam?"

"Why, that would be very kind." She would be sitting down

when he broke the news. It must be concerning Ralph. What else could it be? Perhaps she had misjudged this kind man. To be a gamester was not necessarily to be a monster. Quite respectable men played nowadays. What scrape had her boy got into? He must have broken his promise and this decent gentleman was trying to spare a mother's pain.

Until they had been served she could make small talk, no more, though the maidservant was standing at the edge of the teagarden well out of hearing. Lady Christabel felt rather than heard the tremor in her own voice as she finally was able to ask, "It is about my son Ralph, is it not? Ralph is in some sort of difficulty?"

Mr. Filer seemed astonished. "Ralph? Why, no, madam."

Immediately the tension began to drain from her body and she could smile at the man across the table. An unfortunate face; rather a foxy look, she observed, paying close attention to his appearance for the first time. Nice on a fox, even rather pretty, but untrustworthy on a man they used to say. Poor man, he could not help his looks. And he seemed still very diffident.

"What is it, then, Mr. Filer? Does your concern involve another member of my family?"

He cleared his throat. "To be true, Lady Mawson, I must say that it concerns you yourself, begging your pardon."

"Concerns me?" She knit her brows. "Whatever can you mean?"

He was all concern and apologetic flurry. "Now, now, pray do not let me upset you. What I have to say is of no very great matter. Actually, I thought I might be in a position to be of some small service to you."

Christabel was all at sea. "To me, Mr. Filer?" And then she knew to what he referred. "It is Mr. Carlisle, isn't it? He asked you to speak to me. I must confess, Mr. Filer, it is a great relief to talk to someone about it. I have never done such a thing before, not ever, and it is a very great sum of money. I hardly know where to turn."

"Not so great as all that, Lady Mawson. I am sure you will

find a place to get it." He paused, seeming to consider. "And, as you know, time is of the essence, isn't it?"

"Is it?" she asked. "Surely, Carlisle will understand that I am good for my debt?"

"Mr. Carlisle is a businessman, madam. He may not care to wait."

"He may be forced to," she said, rather more sharply than she had intended. "Surely, there are rules about such things?" She began to feel a small lump of panic begin to build, constricting her throat. "Surely there are rules?" she repeated.

Filer shook his head slowly from side to side. "I fear, dear lady, that they operate in the other direction. No one forced you to wager at Mr. Carlisle's table and the rules say that it is not the *done* thing to wager if you have no way of covering your wager. As you know, social ruination spreads quickly. Too quickly, I fear, in a small backwater such as Cheyne Spa."

A backwater? And she had thought it a splendid place only a fortnight ago. She forced herself to calm her nerves and still the tremour in her hand. She heard herself asking in a clear, cool voice, "And how are these things handled in London, Mr. Filer?"

"Oh, in various ways. Friends, the sale of some small and unimportant property or jewelry. Moneylenders, of course, are everywhere in London."

"Moneylenders? Is there a moneylender in Cheyne Spa, do you know?"

Filer shrugged. "I know of two, but they would ask something of equal value to hold in pawn, you see. Do you have something to give them?"

Miserably she answered that she had not.

"There *is* another way." She was not even looking at him, but she could hear a certain tension in his voice. "You could borrow it from friends."

"I have no friends in Cheyne Spa who are in a position to do so, except the duke and I *could* not ask him. It would destroy too much of the past."

"It is always wise to keep our memories unblemished," he agreed. "No, I was thinking that you could borrow the sum from me. I know, I know, we are not close friends, but I flatter myself that your son, Ralph, has become as a son to me, and I would not like to see him in the distress I know this unfortunate incident would cause him."

Christabel's mind grew very critical of what she was entering upon. To appease it, she asked, "What are your terms, Mr. Filer?"

The gamester was all innocence. "Terms, Lady Mawson? There are no terms. I have just explained my reasoning to you."

"You ask no interest on this money?"

"None whatsoever. And you shall pay me when it is convenient."

Christabel could have wept with relief. She did not know she had bottled it up so inside, but now the crisis was past she knew how it had worried her.

"You are a very generous man, sir."

"It is easy to be generous with such small sums, madam. Pray, you do not worry yourself about it. It is enough that I know my friend, your son, will not be unduly harassed.

"But, Lady Mawson . . ." he held up a cautionary finger. "I think I would avoid the Lower Rooms, if I were you."

"Oh, yes," she said fervently. "Oh, I certainly shall avoid the Lower Rooms in future."

= 23 =

"THERE IS MAMA taking tea with a gentleman." Elizabeth Mawson, armed with her late father's spyglass, gazed across the park from her window. "It is Mr. Filer, I think." She spied also, beyond that, the usual foursome consisting of Lady Barbara, the countess, her own brother, Jack, and Mr. Gerald Wetherbridge, strolling beneath the German lindens. The agony which rent Elizabeth's heart had nothing to do with any real envy of Lady Barbara's beauty, which was undoubtedly an act of God, nor that she and Hermione had been subtly excluded from their company, but with the aching rage of seeing the hand of Mr. Wetherbridge beneath Lady Barbara's elbow.

"I can see the four of them," she told Hermione, "and Mr. Wetherbridge is touching Lady Barbara's arm."

"Do come away," begged her sister with sympathy. "You will only make yourself ill. There are as many fish in the sea as ever came out, I believe. What good does it do to break your heart over a man who has scarcely noticed you and would not recognise you if you spoke to him? . . . Mr. Filer with Mamá?"

Elizabeth, usually too clever for infatuations, agreed in principle, but she did not wish to hear this, since it could not curtail her agony.

"Do you think he might remain unmarried until our come-out, Hermione?"

"I cannot see what difference it would make. He has no money. I heard Mamá say so." Sisters are often unwittingly cruel.

"But he has *position*! He is the duke's great friend and with such influence, who knows how far he might rise? I daresay he has a great future."

Which was, coincidentally, much the same thing that Gerald was at that moment explaining to Lady Barbara, having already mentioned that she held his heart in her hand. Lady Barbara took this as her due, to her credit wearing it gracefully, but she felt compelled, in all compassion, to disabuse him of any hopes in the matter.

"I may even achieve Parliament one day."

"It is true that I hold you in the highest esteem, sir, but it is distinctly improper that you should be saying such things to me." She announced all this so glibly that it was obvious she had said it many times before. But this time she made an addition to the speech out of kindness. "If you have a serious proposal to make it should, I believe, be addressed to my aunt."

Gerald was ecstatic. "Do you mean . . . I say, when may I speak to her?"

Lady Barbara remained demure but firm. "You may certainly speak to her at any time you like, I am sure, but, dear Mr. Wetherbridge, I feel bound to tell you that I could not possibly entertain a *tendre* nor the notion of marriage to any person of your financial prospects. I hope you understand that I must think of my future."

Gerald was taken aback completely, and could only stammer uncomfortably. "But I have already explained that. My future is splendid."

Barbara's demeanour was tender, but her core was adamantine. "Nevertheless, Mr. Wetherbridge, you must consider my position. I am not so placed that I can rest my future on your patron's regard for you." Her tone was kindness itself. "I regret if I injure you, but I would not care to give you false hopes."

"Very thoughtful," said Gerald glumly, "I am sure."

Countess Lavinia and Jack Mawson, who could hardly help knowing the tenor of this conversation, gave Gerald looks of deep sympathy, but Lavinia especially understood Barbara's point of view. Beauty was too ephemeral a quality to waste in waiting for a young man to make his name. Marriage to a poor man would be of no benefit to her, and the possession of a too beautiful wife would be less of advantage than detriment to a young man who had yet to make his way in the world, even one whose patron was the Duke of Towans. Better that he should find a young woman of less beauty but greater cleverness than Lady Barbara enjoyed.

Only Lavinia knew that Barbara had set her sights on the duke himself.

Meanwhile Lady Christabel was reluctantly about to pay a call. Happily, it was not Branston who answered the door of Lady Augusta's house, but Cora, the housemaid, and she, too new and too shy to be anything but deferential, was exactly what Lady Christabel envisioned a housemaid should be.

"What is your name, girl?" Lady Mawson asked.

The little maid curtsied deferentially. "Cora, please, your ladyship."

Her answer piqued Christabel's interest. "You know who I am, then?"

Another curtsey. "Oh, yes, milady."

Christabel preened a bit mentally. If even the servant girls know one's identity, *some* impression must have been made upon the town. "And how is that?"

Cora's eyes drifted over Christabel's shoulder. "Mary is my sister, milady."

"Mary? Who is Mary?"

"I am an' it please your ladyship," said her own maid from behind her.

"Oh, yes. Yes, of course." Not so very interesting, after all.

"Well, Cora, run along and announce me to your mistress. Mary, you may wait in the servant's hall, I daresay, until you are wanted." No need to have the girl hanging about and listening to every word that was said.

Both maids scuttled off like identical white mice.

Christabel looked carefully about the darkish drawing-room with its eclectic furnishings, then settled carefully into a caned bergère. Mostly the apartment reflected the same nondescript taste of her own and other hired houses, but here and there she thought she recognised a piece from Pentreath.

She remained in her chair when her hostess came in.

"Well, Christabel, this is a surprise. I could hardly believe my ears when Cora announced you so unexpectedly. Does this imply a cessation of hostilities?"

"We are not at war, Cousin. I am sure there have never been any pronounced irregularities between us that could not be accounted for by differences of character. You have your little ways and I have mine." Somehow, though, she managed to suggest the implicit superiority of her own mode of behaviour.

"May I offer you refreshment?"

Christabel thought of that most gratifying dish of tea in the public gardens, but decided a second cup would do no harm, although she had no wish to overstimulate herself. They chatted about social trivialities in an amiable fashion until Cora arrived with the tea-tray and retired. Then they settled down to their discussion.

"I daresay you can imagine why I have come," Christabel began.

Her cousin arched her eyebrows in assent, but said nothing.

"My Jack and your Lavinia appear to have formed some sort of mutual attraction. I thought it my business to bring you the news of it before it has progressed further."

"To what point?"

Christabel was nonplussed. "Why, my dear, to discuss the suitability of such an arrangement."

Was the flash in Lady Augusta's eyes a spark or merely an amused twinkle?

"Do you mean to enquire into the background of the *countess*?" The emphasis on the title was faint but evident. "I believe you are well acquainted with her antecedents. I should think that since her father's line was elevated enough for you to very nearly marry him, you would deem hers proper for your son."

Nothing was said of the unfortunate episode which led to the breach of that old engagement, but it was implicit that Lady

Christabel had taken a slight step down by marrying a younger son.

Christabel was not cowed. "Things were rather different then, were they not? Pentreath still stood and the extent of the holdings was, I believe, rather greater. What dowry does the girl bring?"

Lady Augusta, recognising an offensive when she saw one, faced her down. "The rents from the Pentreath land are hers outright, of course, and my own legacy passes to her at my demise as things stand now."

"My dear Augusta, what on earth does that mean?" Lady Christabel laughed merrily. "I hope you do not intend to begin producing heirs at your age?"

Augusta smiled but kept her own counsel on the matter.

"Has your Jack actually made a declaration to the countess?"

And for once Lady Christabel answered frankly. "I really do not know. I had thought perhaps you might be privy to that information. I daresay the girls confide in you rather more quickly than Jack would to his mother, that being the way of men."

"Well, I have heard nothing."

Lady Christabel was obviously taken aback. "Nothing at all?"

"No, nothing. I have used my eyes, though, and I have noted that they seem to incline toward each other, but to my knowledge there has been nothing definite."

A snort of annoyance from the visitor. "But what do you *think*? I have never known you to be without an opinion in any matter."

A sharp thrust, that, but no wound taken.

"I fear you have caught me unprepared, Cousin. I have no answer for your question."

"But what of the suitability of such a match? I know you have considered it."

Lady Augusta considered her words, choosing carefully. "To be straightforward, on the whole I am against it."

Christabel's mouth made a little round O. "Really? My word!"

"If I had thought to marry Lavinia to a farmer, I could as well have stayed in Penwith and saved a great deal of trouble all round."

"The Fogg's Hall estate is nothing to be sneezed at!"

"I do not pretend that it is, Cousin, but I had hoped for a title to match her own."

Finding herself crowded into an unexpected corner, Christabel took refuge in false sentiment. "I believe you would break that child's heart without a qualm."

Augusta smiled calmly. "Not at all. If there is a *tendre* there I will not stand in the way, but I have my views on the matter, as you have suggested."

"I am anxious to hear them."

Lady Augusta remained amiable. "I hope you will be still pleased when I have done. Put simply, my view of the matter is this: there is a diminution of Pentreath land due to my brother's excesses, as you mention. But to weigh in the other direction, there is the title, which would pass, though not to your son, to your grandchildren and their descendants." Here Lady Christabel gave a little shudder as if shunning the idea of grandchildren. "I know that your son's holdings are extensive, for I have made it my business to investigate the matter, and I know, further, that this is largely due to your own management of the estate."

Christabel beamed modestly at being so recognised. "And so, you think, we balance off one against the other?"

Lady Augusta nodded agreement. "Yes, a *good* balance if the two truly care for each other. I would have hoped for a higher estate for my ward, as I said, but I would not stand in the way of true love, if such exists." She drummed her fingers on the chair arm. "I think we must wait and say nothing."

"Oh, but . . . well, if you think best." There could be, then, no borrowing from the estate quite yet. She did not mean to make it seem to be a condition of her blessing. She reached for her shawl of Amiens lace and settled it about her shoulders, but her cousin was not quite done.

"Tell me something further, if you will," Augusta said and Christabel assumed a look of willing patience. "How, may I ask, do you envision your own role on the estate should they decide to marry?"

It was a bold question and Christabel equivocated. "How do you mean?"

"You have managed the Fogg's Hall interests for many years. I believe that Jack has left such matters in your hands, has he not?"

"To a large degree."

"Could you allow the management to pass to someone else?"

A kind of shadow appeared in Christabel's eyes. "I wonder how I shall feel, you know. I admit that it will be difficult to remain merely as an advisor, but I have always known this must happen one day. But they will be in the dower house, after all, and it should not be too difficult."

"Surely, you mistake yourself. *They* will be in the dower house?"

Lady Christabel blushed and stammered. "How stupid of me. I beg your pardon, for I meant to say that *I* will be in the dower house and therefore out of the centre of things. What a silly mistake."

Mistake or not, it left Lady Augusta wondering just what her cousin meant to do? Still, as they had decided, they must first wait to see what the young lovers would choose to do. It must be the decision of Lavvy and Jack alone.

— 24 —

THE MAD VICAR and his passenger rattled into Cheyne Spa at two o'clock of the afternoon and Withering, feeling his muscles might be atrophied, climbed down very carefully. He was not certain whether he would have preferred to travel less hectically now that they were here at last. Racy the curricle might be, it was not constructed for comfortable long-distance journeying. Strangely, Falsworth seemed unaffected and leapt down like a boy.

They were greeted by the usual clangor of bells and the importunities of page-boys and porters, but few, very few beggars for such were banned by law from the watering spot. At Withering's insistence they found lodging not at the Grand Hotel, Falsworth's choice, but at a small, private hotel run by a widow and her daughter. The chambers—separate by the decision of both—were smallish in size, but scrupulously clean. The daughter, the vicar noted, was pretty and plump with only the small defect of a cast in one eye. She quickly brought water for a French bath to dispose of the road dust and within an hour and a quarter the gentlemen were taking tea in St. Gerran's Gardens.

The vicar, ever enthusiastic, fairly bubbled. "I say, Withering, ain't this something? Did you ever think two days ago that you should be taking tea in Cheyne today?"

"No," said his companion thankfully and shifted carefully in his chair. After such an abominable ordeal he was not sure that he would ever sit comfortably again.

"How d'you suppose we go about locating Lady Augusta and company?" the vicar rattled on. "I daresay if we hang about the

Pump Room and make a few discreet inquiries, we shall find them sooner or later, eh?"

"That is something we could do," said his companion dryly, "but I expect it would be considerably quicker and of less distraction to go directly to the house her ladyship has taken."

"Ho, you sly dog, you had the direction all this time? What a rogue you are!"

"I am, after all, the lady's lawyer. It is quite natural that she should communicate to me her whereabouts."

"And I am her spiritual advisor. One can see the relative positions of God and Mammon in all this," the vicar whined in mock petulance.

"Faugh!" was the legal rejoinder.

They had not been sitting there more than ten minutes, sipping the bohea, admiring the excellent layout of the gardens (which, though inferior to the gardens of Cornwall, were nevertheless handsome) and, in the case of the churchman, ogling the young women in their white summer dresses, when they observed something which entirely changed the object of their visit.

"I say, Withering, look there!"

When the lawyer turned his head in the direction his companion indicated he felt his heart drop with sickening speed to the pit of his stomach. There was the object of his adoration, Lady Barbara Pentreath, in such easy conversation with a stalwart and handsome young man that there could be no doubt in the legal mind that they were on terms of the greatest social intimacy. Not that he inferred anything in the least improper, for there, just behind the couple, were Countess Lavinia and another gentleman.

Unable to prevent himself, he summoned their nearby waiter and put to him the question of identification.

"The 'andsome young gent, sir, with Lady Barbara? Sweet on 'er, I expect 'ee is. I know I would be. But they do say she 'as 'er sights set considerable 'igher, if you takes my meaning."

"I don't, actually."

"Well, then, sir, the young man is the ward of the Duke of

Towans, ain't 'ee?" His voice dropped conspiratorially. "Though there be some as suggests a closer family tie, if you takes my meaning now. Any old way they says that whichever she catches, the lord or the ward, she'll be flyin' 'igh, y'know."

Then, seeing the stricken look upon his customer's face he asked anxiously. " 'Ere, I ain't given you bad news, I 'opes? Is the couple known to you then, sir?"

"Only my deuced curiosity," said Withering valiantly. "The young ladies are neighbours, you know, from home." He set the teacup down very carefully to disguise the tremor of his hand. "The young ladies are very popular here, are they?"

"You might so say, sir!" the waiter replied enthusiastically. "Quite the rage, they is, in their different ways. Such a difference between 'em, but not an inch to choose in the swim. They often sits at my tables," he said proudly as if their celebrity were somehow contagious.

"And who is the other gentleman?" asked the vicar.

"Name of Mawson, sir. Young landowner hereabouts."

"I see. Well off, is he?"

The waiter chuckled. "You might say that, sir. Yes, I believe you might say that of probably the very what the Bible calls 'rich young ruler' of the area. Yes, I would say well off." Still chuckling he offered his service to another table.

The two men looked glumly at each other. Withering perceived that Barbara was beyond him. Was he just at that age, he wondered, when men are exceptionally vulnerable to lovely young women? Well, there was no harm in it, though he had very nearly made a great fool of himself. What was that play of Sheridan's? *School For Scandal*? How he had laughed at the old husband being mocked by the young wife. It did not seem so merry now. He gave a great, gusty sigh of mingled regret and relief. Yes, well out of it.

"Needn't have hurried, eh?" asked the vicar. "Or perhaps we should have begun our journey sooner." He was taking it very serenely, as though he had not been very much engaged in the matter of the heart. Perhaps he had not, thought Withering in a savage moment. Perhaps the constant jolting of his blasted high-perch curricle had addled his brains.

Throwing down some money he arose from the table.

"I say, Withering, where are you off to?"

But Young Withering merely strode away with a straight back and very still shoulders.

Lady Augusta Mabyn's second caller of the day was a very great surprise. When Cora, trembling with anxiety, came to the breakfast room she threw Branston's mistress and the manservant into an instant panic. The usually imperturbable Branston was particularly affected.

"My word, milady, His Royal Highness here? What should we do?"

"Do? We must welcome him, I suppose." In reality Augusta wanted nothing so much as to take flight through the rear courtyard and sit in St. Gerrans's Gardens until he had gone away.

But she knew she could not do that. A sense of imminent doom swept over her.

"Oh, Branston, what on earth do you suppose he wants?"

A tall plump figure filled the doorway. "What I would like, Lady Augusta, if I may be so bold, is a dish of bohea."

She slid automatically into a deep curtsey. "Your Royal Highness has taken us by surprise."

"Here, here, none of that. A mere suppliant has no right to such courtesies." He gestured delicately at Branston and at Cora who, backed against the wall, was stricken with awe and terror at the proximity of such a god.

"Branston, be so good as to take Cora into the kitchen and then prepare . . ." she turned back to the Prince ". . . You would not prefer coffee, sir, or perhaps a glass of Cornish mead?"

The Prince was delighted. "You have meth Kernewek? What a pleasure. Of course, I shall have some of it!" He looked about him and selected a sturdy Jacobean chair.

"Oh, sir, you will not be very comfortable."

The Prince smiled and crinkles of amusement formed about his eyes.

"Heppelwhite is a bit delicate for a man of my size, I fear. I shall feel more secure in this."

Settling in, he clasped his hands loosely across his abdomen and inclined his head graciously. Lady Augusta sat, but made a mental note that the furnishing of the front salons should include seating on a somewhat coarser scale to accommodate patrons of varying size.

For a few moments they conversed lightly about the weather, the season, the spa, and, when it was brought and sipped out of delicately fluted glasses, the Cornish mead.

The Prince, who was also by right the Duke of Cornwall, smacked his lips appreciatively. "But there is a faint and subtle difference from the meth I recall," he commented.

"I hope it does not displease you, sir?"

"On the contrary. Pray, what have you done?"

Lady Augusta had taken great pride in the still-room at Pentreath and she was pleased at the perception of her guest. Yes, as Towans had said to her, the man had great charm.

"A small variation of my own, sir. The sap of the birch was substituted for a portion of the water in the receipt."

"Interesting. I daresay you must miss Cornwall a great deal and Pentreath in particular. I visited there once a long while ago when I was just a boy. Fine old house, as I remember. Is it completely gone?"

"Completely, sir."

"What a pity. I remember that you used to have a great ball there at Yuletide."

"Yes, sir, but no more. Those days are lost, I am afraid."

Now she saw how he was approaching his subject as he asked, "I daresay the balls in the Upper Rooms are poor stuff by comparison, eh?"

"I believe Your Highness has quite revolutionised the habits of those who attend them."

"Ummm. For the better, I hope. I know the old minuet has long been a staple of gentility . . . for an age, I daresay . . . but, really, the waltz is far more amusing, do you not agree?" He took the liberty of pouring more of the mead. "Such a pleasure, such a pleasure."

His hostess knew *she* could not broach an inquiry concerning the purpose of his visit, but he continued to make inconsequential conversation while she mentally fidgeted in her chair. At last, without ever having mentioned anything more stirring than the nearby scenery, he rose from his chair, very lightly for such a large man.

"Well, I must be about my business. Going up and down upon the face of the earth, I am sure some would say."

Augusta began to curtsey, but he forstalled her. "No, no, enough of formality." He turned toward the door, then back to her with a false air of impromptu.

"By the by, Lady Augusta, I feel I must commend you upon your behaviour at the recent gathering in the Upper Rooms, and to thank you most expressly for your graciousness to Mrs. Fitzherbert. I am only sorry I was not present to witness it."

And well he might, thought his hostess, since Mrs. Fitz had left him cooling his heels at the front while she slipped out the back of her house.

"I felt it my duty, Your Highness. Mrs. Fitzherbert is a lady of great charm and worth."

His face was sad and reflective. Also a bit cunning, she thought. What was coming next?

"Yes, she is that. Very charming and very worthy. I am glad you found that in her."

Again he turned toward the door, again Lady Augusta prepared to curtsey him out and summon Branston. And again he turned back. It was theatrically done with no pretense of subtlety whatsoever.

"I understand that you will, in a few days, be preparing a small celebration of a friend's birthday. May I presume to be included?"

This time she curtsied to save showing her annoyance, but not before she took note of the gleam of triumph in his eyes. "We will be honoured by your presence, sir."

She tugged the bellrope sharply.

═ 25 ═

IT WAS VERY odd, Elizabeth thought, that it was she who usually slipped away from Hermione for a few moments to herself, but that this time it was Hermione who had wandered away from *her*. It was not that she felt anything dreadful would befall her sister, but that, really, she was not at all sure that it was actually the first time it had happened. It might be that, once or twice of the times she had believed she was eluding Hermione, exactly the reverse was true.

In any case, Hermione was nowhere to be seen.

Elizabeth began to wander about St. Gerrans's Gardens and, not for the first time, realised that she was becoming too old to do so alone, no matter what her private inclinations. More than one young man shot her a flashing smile and a rougish look; more than one older gentleman tipped his hat and tried to engage her in conversation. It was frustrating to find that she could no longer sit quietly and observe the world as it went by without danger of being accosted. The fate of being a proper young woman was ready to descend upon her and it was a great pity. Why could life not go on in the same way it had always done, save better and freer? What was the advantage of growing up if one had always to be bound by attitudes and rules set down by other people?

She passed the great fountain, one of Hermione's favourite spots, with its strong jets of water shooting up amidst the gilded statuary of Diana and her hounds pulling down poor Actaeon; she crossed the street and peered into the shops where Hermione always lingered: the bookseller's, the shop of the little modiste who had been, she said, an *aristo* in Paris, and the shop where ribbons and laces of all sorts were to be seen, and paused at the offerings of the glovemaker. But no Hermione.

At last, in desperation, she crossed again to the gardens, determined to peep inside the tea garden, though Hermione would never venture there alone, but just as she reached the entrance there was Hermione at her side.

"Elizabeth! You naughty child, where have you been? I've been looking all over." But this was said without any real conviction and with a sort of downcast, eye-sliding look. For the first time Elizabeth believed her sister was lying to her. Where had she been? Dared she ask Hermione, who had always been kind about not asking *her* where she had been?

But if she had asked, Elizabeth would have told her.

As they moved away from the entrance to the tea garden a man came out whom Elizabeth recognized as someone she believed to be called Filer. He was the man she had seen having tea with her mother earlier in the day. What a curious coincidence! The man must all but *live* in the tea garden. He gave the young women a slight bow and a half smile, then turned to walk in the other direction. Elizabeth was holding on to her sister's arm, and was surprised to find that Hermione was trembling.

"Sister, are you not well?"

"Only a little tired. Shall we go back to the lodging?"

To her sister, Hermione did not look tired at all, but, really, rather radiant. It was all very perplexing.

As they turned to go, Mr. Beau Carlisle came out of the garden.

Lady Augusta found that preparations for the birthday party were, of necessity, elaborate. Branston was right, the acceptances poured in. No one who valued their social standing would dream of denying themselves the promise of the party of the season.

"Dare we hope," Lady Augusta asked dispairingly of Branston, "that some will arrive early and leave early?"

Branston's sense of irony was most in evidence. "I think you may assume, madam, that many will arrive early and stay until the very end."

"Oh, dear, I think we have succeeded too well."

Cora entered with a harried expression. "If you please, mum, the men have arrived with the gaming tables." She turned to go, then distractedly contrite to have forgotten, she added, "And, beggin' your pardon, mum, Mr. Carlisle is in the yellow sitting room."

"Carlisle, oh, dear. Branston, would you . . . no, perhaps I'll see him."

She went into the front of the house and found Beau Carlisle, not in the yellow room, but directing the men in setting up the tables. His sleeves were turned back so that the lace would not catch, and he was working alongside them with a will.

"No, no, not that way, dolts. The light from the chandelier will be directly in the dealer's eyes. Rotate the table slightly. That is it!" He saw that Lady Augusta was watching with amusement.

"I thought it only right to give you the benefit of my experience. I hope you don't mind."

She looked with surprise at the face which, stripped of its maquillage and patches, had an open, almost boyish quality. She surmised that at some time in the past Beau Carlisle had been something of a natural heartbreaker.

"But only two tables?" he asked. "You can't fly high with that, dear lady."

"These tables are to be only a diversion at the duke's party for those who are not musical," she explained. "I fear that there will be such a crush that even this will be useless."

He nodded understandingly. "Yet they . . . the future patrons, I mean . . . will know they are here. I congratulate you on your novel way of introducing the enterprise. It lends a cachet mere money could never buy."

"I shall expect *you* to oversee much on the birthday. Though I would care to, I know I shall be besieged, the indications are already evident."

He looked at her obliquely. "I, madam? I shall not be here. Mine is, perhaps, the one invitation returned with regret."

She was perplexed. "But our arrangement . . ."

"Is, I fear, void, Lady Augusta. I take the liberty of confiding in you as a professional courtesy that I made rather a large wager last evening and, happily, won. I think it is time I severed my ties with Cheyne Spa."

"But in real fact you *are* Cheyne Spa. What it is has always been by your design."

"True," he said a little huskily, "and I do not pretend to you that I have not enjoyed my glory. But," he shrugged, "all things end."

"And our arrangement?"

"Luckily, it has never begun. But, should you choose to go on with your scheme, you would have no real need of me. After the birthday celebration you will have Cheyne Spa at your feet to do with them what you will."

"Where will you go?"

She had never seen him grin before, only give controlled smiles. He spread his hands as if the fates were his only future mentors. "That has not, alas, been revealed to me. Somewhere quiet, I expect, where I can do penance without drawing undue attention." His laugh had a hollow sound.

Lady Augusta could not help asking compassionately, "Are you in some difficulty, sir?"

His laugh was a short, dismissing bark. "No. Have I not told you I made a rather sweet killing? I think it best to close up shop before it is squandered away. Money and cards slip through my fingers with equal ease."

He presently bade her good-bye and departed, not without again wishing her all good fortune. The visit left her pensive for a moment, but she had too much to accomplish to dwell long upon it.

Gerald Wetherbridge had little to occupy his time since the lady of his heart had so certainly explained to him that he was not remotely eligible for her regard. It had not surprised him when he heard the news, but it had punctured his dreams with acerbic finality, leaving the withered taste of them upon his tongue like aloes. There is nothing quite so melancholy as an impractical dream come to dust, as most of us know, but which the majority of us find it difficult to accept. Pretty maids and lads come and go and their leavetaking often leaves us bereft.

Luckily he had intelligence that the duke would be returning from London by dinnertime, which cheered the youth somewhat. He admired and genuinely liked his employer, whose company had always been an education in acquiring that polished view of the world without which urbanity is a shell. The breadth of the duke's interests, appetites and education, both physical and intellectual, impressed him as greatly worthy of emulation. He would be glad to be in Towans's company again, but meanwhile the time rather dragged, for slow-time in youth is very slow indeed. Therefore it was with a sense of gratitude that he replied to the summons of a heavy knocking upon the door of the duke's apartments. The young man who stood there was known to him slightly, more by sight than conversation, but he invited him to enter and share a pipe.

"I have actually come to importune the duke," said Ralph Mawson. "Do you think he would consent to see me?"

Gerald explained that his grace would not return until evening, "But you seem a largish bit overwrought, old fellow. Isn't there something I can do? Sometimes even talking about a problem shows a way out of it."

"I wouldn't care to trouble *you* with it. I've got myself into a deuced pickle and no mistake. I cannot go to my brother at the moment, and I can't turn to my mother without more recrimination than I care to endure."

"Money, is it? I have a little to offer you if you'll take it."

"It'll take considerably more than 'a little', I'm afraid." He put his head in his hands and rocked back and forth. "Oh, I have been a stupid fool and no joke."

"You're skint?"

"Completely. There is this man named Filer. Perhaps you've heard of him."

"I believe I have," said Gerald without commenting further.

"Then perhaps you know he is a professional gambler? A sharp, really."

"You got mixed up with him?"

Ralph could only nod. "He's had me running about for days now, trying to raise the money, but I've had no luck. None at all. They seem to be used to bankrupts in this town. You'd think I was a leper and contagious. The duke was my last hope. I thought that since he and my mother were friends . . ."

"Are they? I didn't know that."

"So Mam says, children together, I believe." He was obviously not much interested in his mother's childhood. Instead he stood up and turned out his pockets dramatically.

"I gather he's wrung you dry?" asked Gerald. "Perhaps a little more than dry?"

"I am afraid so. I know I sound an awful 'sap', don't I, but, you see . . . he was so amiable."

"I am sure you were not the first to be taken in. You thought he was your friend?"

Ralph considered that. "No, not exactly. I mean, I knew he was a gambler, that he made his living at it. He made no secret of that. But I thought . . . I don't know what I thought."

"That he was a gentleman?"

Gerald's precise questions were obviously riling Ralph and he answered shortly. "I say, gentlemen *do* play cards, you know!" Then, ruefully, "I even sound like a fool to myself, forgive me."

"What I don't understand," said Gerald, "is why you didn't stop when you ran out of money?"

"You don't gamble, do you?" said Ralph as if talking to someone a little dim. "I kept thinking my luck would change and that I'd win it all back and the other lot as well."

"He'd been into you before? How much?"

"Quite a lot, actually. My mother, Lady Mawson, paid off that."

Gerald shook his head disbelievingly. "On what conditions?"

"What do you mean? She's my mother!"

"Have it your way," said Gerald. "I've never yet seen a mother who couldn't drive a harder bargain than a banker. It was on condition that you give up gambling, wasn't it? Or at least that you abstain until you reach your majority?" He said it as kindly and understandingly as he knew how to do, but Ralph was so beaten down that he merely hung his head abjectly and would not answer. "Where did you get the money to begin a second time?"

"I hadn't any. Filer let me play on credit. Actually, I won a lot of it back at first. I thought I was going to be all right, you see. I had had a run and built up my stake until I could almost repay Mam."

"And then he took it back and led you deeper, eh?"

Faced with the logic of it, Ralph was close to tears. "My brother'll kill, just kill me. He warned me off it not a month ago. He has no sympathy for gaming, just lives for the hounds and horses." He stood up and walked aimlessly about the room. "Jack is a good chap, don't mistake me. Probably a lucky thing he got the inheritance." He held out his hand to Gerald. "I think I won't bother the duke, after all. You've done me a world of good, Wetherbridge. I'll remember it. Do you as good a turn one day, I hope."

Gerald clapped him about the shoulder man to man. "What will you do?"

"Go to my brother, I expect. I imagine that is the best thing, contain it within the family no matter what.".

"Yes," Gerald agreed, "it probably is."

Funny, he thought, when Mawson had come in he had thought him pretty wet, but now . . . well, dash it, now he found he rather liked him. He did wonder, though, why, if Filer had been leading Ralph along all this time with the promise of easy money, he had suddenly begun turning the screws. It didn't seem quite logical, did it?

═ 26 ═

WHAT HIS GRACE the Duke of Towans said when he returned to Cheyne Spa to find himself the centerpiece of a social maelstrom is not recorded. Probably, since he was not an angel, he let slip a great many unguarded words, but also, since he was essentially amiable and, as we have seen, tolerably fond of the lady who was sponsoring the event, he may have said them only to Gerald.

At any rate, all seemed well enough until the mid-afternoon of the day in question. There is a tradition which says that the bridegroom should not see the bride on her wedding day until that moment when she stands beside him. It might be, as well, for the sake of those of a ducal nature, to extend that tradition and announce that the guest of honour should never be allowed to see the preparations until the festivities have begun. It might save a deal of trouble.

In honest fact the dreary house had been transformed, with the combined efforts of Branston, Cora, and a host of subsidiary in-and-outers, to a veritable palace in miniature. The walls had been painted, new carpets laid down and the chandeliers taken apart and each brilliant bathed and polished to the utmost, then rehung. The furniture was sparse to allow for the expected crush, but in the little salon opposite the yellow sitting room, the gaming tables were set up, decks and boxes laid out as if play might at any time begin.

The duke was not amused.

He had not much personal ego, but a great deal of family pride and an awareness of what is due rank. Both were affronted. Lady Augusta at first pretended that he was merely being tetchy.

"Oh, come, my dear, are you going to force respectability on me? I vow, I have had such a taste of the other that I may never in this life be respectable again."

"I would prefer you to take the tables away for this one night, if you please."

"But why? You know what I plan to do here. Be glad that I am not throwing the doors open to the public at large. Be reasonable, Towans," she pleaded. "What are your objections?"

"I object, madam, because I see myself as the lure for gulls. Could you not have waited one night?"

"And lost the impetus? You ask too much. Towans, these are only two of ten tables that will occupy these rooms. I have not devised a gambling hell for your dishonour, after all. Only two tables for those who are not musical and will not appreciate Faltinelli. They must have some diversion, after all."

He said nothing more, but the look he offered her was chill and he made his departure abruptly.

Lavinia came in just as he was leaving. "Was that not the duke, Aunt? He rushed straight past without seeing me. Did he like the preparations for his party?"

Augusta told her of their dispute.

"Will you take the tables away?" She looked a bit worried. "He *will* come back, won't he?"

"I honestly cannot say. I imagine he will escort Mrs. Fitzherbert."

"Did you warn him of the way the Prince forced an invitation?"

"I had no chance. I daresay he will find it out quickly enough."

She wandered about the house in a fit of agitation. She had come to realise how dear Towans was to her both as friend and sponsor. Could she afford to test that relationship?

Resignedly she closed the doors of the salon, wrote a brief note and rang for Cora to run it round to the duke's apartments. There would be other evenings for play.

And with the settling of dusk the fifty-odd began to arrive in twos and threes, while a crowd of the less fortunate collected outside the gate to watch and wait. It was something, after all, to have been there, even if one was not allowed inside. And perhaps it would be possible to enjoy the music through the open windows. Pity the poor hostess who had scheduled an affair in opposition to this one. There would be no contest at all.

However, Elizabeth Mawson felt it best to consult with her mother in the midst of family preparations. "I think you had better speak to Hermione, Mama. I am not at all sure she is well."

Christabel hurried to the chamber the girls shared and found Hermione lying on her bed with a damp cloth across her eyes.

"What is it, my dear? A headache?"

Hermione waved a hand languidly. "It is nothing, Mamá. A slight indisposition. I shall get up presently."

Her mother laid her fingers on the girl's cheek. "There seems to be no fever."

The girl impatiently turned her head away. "Forgive me, I cannot bear to be touched. My poor head is throbbing so!"

Christabel surveyed her judiciously. "Perhaps you need a purgative. It has been some time since you last had one." She made as if to locate one, but Hermione moaned and threshed slightly on the bed, disturbing the cover.

"Oh, please, no, Mamá," she begged in a nasal, whining voice, "but if perchance there are headache powders?"

"There are indeed. Elizabeth, fetch them from the cabinet in my chamber." She wore a smug look of satisfaction. It always worked with her children; threaten them with a medicine which they thought dreadful and they would easily settle for a lesser remedy. Even growing up they never changed. She removed the cloth from her daughter's eyes. Hermione sat up.

"You *do* look a trifle green, dearest. Perhaps you should not think of going out tonight?"

The expected protest was feeble. "Oh, no. Once I have the headache remedy I daresay I shall be well enough."

"Just as you like, Hermione. I am sure you are old enough to know whether you will like a noisy, crowded gathering. I cannot think that I should, but perhaps the powders will put you in better spirits."

Something a little like alarm flashed in her daughter's eyes and she lay her head back on the pillow. "I am sure you are right, Mamá. It is just that I hate to offend Aunt Augusta."

Christabel's expression tightened. "I am sure Lady Augusta will do very well with the number of guests she has, without missing a poor, sick girl."

= 27 =

As everyone knew Faltinelli was superb, only those guests who had come principally to gamble were disgruntled, and even they were impressed by the restraint shown by Lady Augusta in closing the gaming room.

"She could so easily have taken advantage of the evening," opined the Duchess of Doddington, "but breeding always tells, does it not? I am sure I wish her all the luck there is with her gaming rooms. So much nicer to play privately than in the crowd of the Lower Rooms."

"Do you play?" someone asked her in surprise, for she was never seen at the tables.

"Oh, dear, no. My words were general, I fear." Her slightly vapid laugh tinkled lightly. "Or, rather . . . I must confess . . . I do enjoy a quiet game of piquet with a congenial opponent." Everyone suspected she meant her famous majordomo. A duchess could not commit social suicide by marrying beneath her, but she could legitimately keep a companion in her employ without outrage.

The castrato took the closure of the room as a personal compliment to his art. "Thees Laddy Agoosta, she ees sensiteev to the arteestic needs! Nevair 'ave I meet weeth more conseederation! All weel come to 'eer Faltinelli . . ." he winked roguishly ". . . whether 'ee choose to or not!" This sally was generally appreciated, even by the gamesters.

Lady Christabel was quick to point out to Elizabeth that she should make a special effort to remember this evening, for who could tell when she would meet Faltinelli's like again. Her son,

Ralph, staying close to her side, agreed with his mam. "Demmed fine singer, Elizabeth." Neither seemed to remember that Elizabeth had already had the pleasure of the singer's artistry in the concert hall. This was, admittedly, quite different, but, honestly, Elizabeth could not say that the earlier concert had been to her taste. She had not the musical education to appreciate by the remnant what a glory the voice must once have been.

Lady Augusta and Lady Barbara mingled throughout the company with an eye toward giving the countess more time with Jack Mawson. Barbara did not mind at all that her sister would marry a landowner, nearly a gentleman farmer, so long as it did not affect her own value on the market, and it was a surprise to many of the guests that she could be so outgoing when she chose, since their earlier glimpses had been through a crowd of young male admirers.

Augusta was astonished, however, to hear the next guest announced. "Mr. Beau Carlisle!"

He was dressed with much the same restraint she had seen on his last visit. No paint, the clothes in rather sombre good taste, his hair unpowdered and carrying no ceremonial staff of office. The mayor saw him at once and moved directly toward him with a stern expression, but Carlisle ostentatiously turned his back and began chatting with the Duchess of Doddington. When he felt Mayor Tobias's hand upon his arm, however, he greeted him with every indication of pleasure.

Tobias's face was a thundercloud. "See here, Carlisle, what are you up to? Why ain't you about the business we pay you for, instead of strutting about at a private party dressed . . ." he surveyed Carlisle's costume contemptuously ". . . like a gravedigger?"

"Nonsense, old fellow, best of taste. Sorry it don't please you, what?"

Tobias gritted his teeth and, leaning forward, said in what he thought to be an undertone, "Dammee, fool, if you value your job you'll do as I tell you to do!" It was overheard by several bystanders and had spread round the room in seconds. And Carlisle waited for it. When he was sure he had every ear he smiled very genially at Mayor Tobias and patted him patronisingly on the shoulder.

"But you see, sir, I do *not* value my job. In fact, sir, I give you leave to offer it to someone else, for I have done with it!" In the wake of this astonishing news he moved to his hostess and bent over her hand.

"You have made quite a stir, Mr. Carlisle," she murmured.

"No more than I had intended, madam." He gestured toward the closed salon. "I see that all my work was done in vain."

"There were, I fear, objections from the guest of honour."

"Stuffy fellow. Always was." He tapped a finger to his brow. "I say, I've just had a capital idea. Why don't you run away with *me*?"

"You *are* going through with it, then?"

"Ah, yes. You'll be rid of *two* rivals. Chap I took the money from is absconding as well. Been collecting his due debts all over the town, I hear." His eyes fell on Lady Christabel who was in conversation with Mrs. MacElroy. "How does one issue a warning to the like of Lady Mawson, do you think?"

"What sort of warning? I suppose you simply go across and give it her."

Carlisle strolled about the room, nodding and bowing, with a smile here and a good word there until he reached the side of Lady Christabel.

Christabel was delighted at his arrival; it set her above the crowd, even though he was going away. Her lips, parted in greeting, froze at his first words. "You have no place here, madam. You had better be at home." This said with a peculiar look of intensity. Christabel hardly knew what to say. It seemed such an audacious bit of gall that it deserved very little. Her nostrils flared, even as her lips grew pinched and she asked in an offended tone, "Are you drunk, sir?" and walked away from him.

Carlisle, however, seemed not about to let this pass. Following in her footsteps he accosted her a second time. "I say to you, again, Lady Mawson, you had better be at home!"

Ralph came to his mother's defense. "See here, sir, I will

thank you not to annoy my mother!" Carlisle quieted him with a look of such supreme superiority that the lad actually quailed back a step. "If you looked after your mother's interests, boy, as she does yours, you would both be better off."

Even Lady Augusta was astonished at this appearance of the utmost in boorish behaviour on the part of one who had been the spa's arbiter of such things. Then she recalled what he had said about *warning* Lady Mawson. Could his seeming rudeness been a calculated message? Not at all disconcerted by his seeming failure Carlisle returned to Lady Augusta's side and bowed again, this time rather deeply.

"I thank you again, my lady, for your acquaintance . . . and your forbearance. I fear my seed fell on stony ground."

Nodding and smile-laden he passed again through the crowd of guests and passed from their lives. And, as out of sight, out of mind, there was a general movement toward the salon where the concert seating had been arranged. Augusta moved to her cousin and linked her arm in hers.

"That *dreadful* man! I cannot think how you allow such people to be your guests," said Christabel indignantly. "A completely unprovoked attack!"

"Is it not possible, Cousin, that he was conveying something *other* than the impertinence you supposed?"

Lady Christabel drew herself up. "What *could* he have meant? I have every right to be here."

"Yes, you do. Every right. All the same, do you not think it wise to set Ralph or Jack to investigate? Where, for instance, is Hermione tonight?"

Luckily, they were the last to leave the room or Lady Mawson's sudden screech of comprehension would have disrupted everyone. Elizabeth, who had been hovering nearby, hurried to her mother's side. The two walked Christabel, supporting her to the empty gaming room, which, since the yellow sitting room had no doors, happened to be the nearest private spot. Christabel moaned pitifully when she saw the accoutrements it contained and put her head on her hand. Elizabeth rummaged in her mother's reticule for smelling salts and Augusta left them together while she sought the two young men and packed them off to the lodging.

Really, it had never seemed so difficult to give a party. And, as yet, the guest of honour had not arrived. She made her way into the salon where the others were waiting. Faltinelli began his recital with one or two Renaissance melodies and started upon the ravishing *Caro mio ben*, but had hardly reached the second line when there was a slight flurry outside in the hall, towards which all heads turned, even the castrato's, though theirs carried expressions of interest and his of annoyance. Presently the doors of the salon were diffidently, almost stealthily opened and the latecomer stepped inside.

It was His Royal Highness, the Prince of Wales.

Augusta hurriedly left her seat and greeted him softly, but he drew her further aside and murmured some question in her ear which the others could not hear, to which she shrugged delicately with those impertinent shoulders and shook her head. This recalled to the guests what had already crossed her mind, that they had not seen the guest of honour whose natal day they were celebrating. Most would have argued that the presence of a Royal Highness was an acceptable substitute.

Faltinelli, in particular, was gratified to the point of offering to begin the program again but the Prince would not hear of it. "*Signore*, I extend my deepest apologies for having disrupted your beautiful music. I shall, I am sure, vastly enjoy the remainder of the program." *Caro mio ben* was abandoned and, when the Prince was seated at the side of Lady Augusta, the recital went on with an ayre of that charming murderer, Gesualdo, though the remainder of the venture was somewhat marred by the inclination of the Prince to crane toward the door at the slightest sound.

As it fell out, his vigilance was not rewarded until the music was concluded and the party preparing to go into supper. The knocker sounded on the outside door, the Prince at once turned toward the sound, and at his benifice the Royal countenance was suffused with an almost radiant joy, for Branston, in his most resonant tones, announced, "His Grace, the Duke of

Towans and . . ." here he paused, though he would never admit it was for effect ". . . Mrs. Fitzherbert!"

The hush upon the room was total. Not a person but hardly dared breathe, much less stir. The Prince all but ran forward, his hands extended and visibly trembling. With a glad cry he slid into a kind of kneeling crouch and with a voice choked with emotion croaked, "Maria!"

Mrs. Fitzherbert said nothing, merely stood there transfixed and with an expression upon her face of deepest remorse. Presently they all knew why. Branston's voice rang out again in stentorian tones, the names of a second pair of guests now entering.

"Mr. Gerald Wetherbridge and . . . Her Royal Highness, Caroline, Princess of Wales!"

There was a very long moment of silence.

The expression growing upon the face of the Prince was a terrible thing to behold. The broken and bereft look of the abandoned child, the disbelief of the man whose treasure has turned to dry leaves in his hand, were cousins-german to this, compounded equally of wretchedness and royalty as he looked from one woman to the other; the loved and unloved wives.

Maria Fitzherbert, tears now streaming from her face, saw what she had done to him. What had begun as a lark, a trick of Mistress Page and Mistress Ford, had become a jest not worth the having. All bitterness. All tears. She had thought to cure him with discomfiture of his fickle passion for her, but nothing, no amorous persecution, was worth this ending. He looked to her so bewildered that she put out her hands and raised him.

"It is over," she said firmly as a mother might say to buck up a child.

The Princess Caroline, plump and rather dowdy for all her fine clothes, had a sly expression about the eyes and an open face that said it could enjoy a good joke. And this was a very, very funny joke was it not? She did not fathom these English. Why was no one laughing? They all disliked her husband; perhaps more than she herself did, but no one laughed. Her sly look deepened. The joke seemed better than before!

Lady Augusta stood frozen as she watched the changing expressions flit across the faces of her guests. Amusement—outrage—disgust. She herself had played the biggest gamble of all—and lost. Her dream of an acceptable gambling salon was shattered. It would never recover from the scandal of this evening. To go on would be to court social oblivion!

— 28 —

THE SOFT AIR of Cornwall's September lay like a blessing upon the countryside. Lady Augusta and her wards were once again living in the house in St. Buryan. None had left the tangled events at Cheyne Spa with anything like regret, though Lady Augusta still considered returning to open the gambling salon next season. Despite the opposition she had met from the duke and, of course, Lady Barbara, the notion had not deserted her. While it was settled that Lavinia would wed Jack Mawson, it was generally agreed that it must wait until Hermione had been found and Filer somehow punished.

It was for the insulting note the scoundrel had left behind him as much as anything else that his brothers-in-law longed to discover him. They had not shown it to their mother, although it was to her it had been addressed.

> *For the sum of £250 in gambling notes,*
> *received, one (1) daughter, willing.*

And across the bottom had been scrawled in large black letters:

PAID IN FULL.

Contrary to past actions, Lady Christabel took it all upon herself. She, it was, who had borrowed money from the wretch to cover her own shame; she who had kept Hermione so ignorant of the ways of life that she would listen to the persuasions of such an odious creature; she, in fact, who had dug the trap for her own downfall.

More and more, Elizabeth found her mother turning to her for comfort, what small comfort she could give. It was more than a little sad that such closeness had only come with adversity. As for Elizabeth herself, the episode, though inglorious, had a certain value, for, as she wrote to Countess Lavinia, it contained a veritable goldmine of material for a practicing novelist such as she had made up her mind to become. Life was, after all, so very interesting when examined dispassionately at one remove. Even the circumstance of her own infatuation with Gerald might, in the interests of literature, prove worthy. Doubtless, there were women who had allowed such things to play havoc with their lives. Look at Phèdre, for example, or that nasty creature Medea.

With Hermione gone and Mama turned into 'Niobe, all tears', it was a decided blessing that she herself and Lavinia, though with few interests in common, were congenial. What a bad thing it would be to live at home with a new sister-in-law whom one found an antidote. She was grateful for Lavvy's letters and responded with her own at each breath of news.

It was through Elizabeth's letters, for example, that Lady Augusta and her nieces learned the unhappy conclusion of the Cheyne Spa affair. The Prince, it appeared, had returned at once to London, carrying with him, no doubt, a great deal of animosity toward all concerned in his humiliation. Particularly, it was thought, toward the Princess of Wales. Mrs. Fitzherbert, according to Elizabeth's sources, had left to resume that nomadic life which her circumstances and restlessness dictated. There were, Elizabeth said, sporadic mentions of her in the press, but one knows how unreliable the press can be.

> As to the Duke of Towans, (she wrote) no one, or at any rate, no one with whom I am acquainted, has any real information at all. Rumours abound, but what is that? Some say he has retired to his old estates in Rutland, some said he was organising an expedition to dig for antiquities in Arabia Deserta, and one tale even has him emigrating to Virginia, where he has

vast holdings in the tidewater region. None, alas, have any substance. To my view the only good things to come out of the sad summer are, naturally, your betrothal, dear Lavvy, to my excellent brother, and the notion, still unconfirmed, that Barbara and I might, after all, share a London comeout next year.

Privately, Lady Augusta worried that the echoes of the Cheyne Spa affair might resound even to London, thus rendering such a debut pointless. Certainly, in the present climate, the Prince would not be pleased to be reminded of his setdown. But she wisely said nothing.

The suggestion, at any rate, pacified Lady Barbara, who might well have become somewhat desperate without it. In the remembrance of her power in Cheyne, her beauty had become nearly an obsession. She lavished hours upon the care of her person and fretted that her bloom might have faded before her vogue had blossomed. Suggestions from her sister and aunt that her peak could hardly have been reached were of no avail and she lived in a state of heightened anxiety.

Once she said to Lady Augusta, all unaware, "I wonder if we shall ever again see the dear duke?" so wistfully that her aunt realised Barbara had never understood the true circumstance, and that the very beauty of which she was so proud, and with it the resemblance to his last duchess, was one of the reasons the duke had no interest in her. There seemed no point in telling her now.

By mid-August Branston (and the new additions to his staff, Cora and her young sister) had reestablished the routines of the St. Buryan household and made it into a home once more. The days passed quietly and without exterior incident until, one early afternoon, a coach-and-four drew up beside the front wall. The matched cream horses were handsome enough to draw exclamations of admiration from the countess and her aunt, but the ladies were quite puzzled when Young Withering climbed down from the interior of the vehicle and walked up the drive toward the house. Lady Augusta, who had seen very little of him since coming home, met him at the door.

He stood there with his hat in his hand for all the world as if he were a near-stranger, and one not entirely in her graces. He seemed uncharacteristically nervous for a lawyer and dropped his eyes when he began speaking.

"I have come, my lady, on a rather difficult errand. There is, within the coach, a person of station who would have a word with you."

"How very surprising," was all her ladyship could think to reply. "Might we not be more comfortable in my parlour?"

Withering shifted his body uncomfortably, almost squirming. "It is a person, madam, who feels the discourse might better be conducted in the coach." He eyed her anxiously. "Will you trust me, Lady Augusta, with this indulgence?"

"Certainly, old friend." She extended her hand and he guided her down the steps; in the drive she walked with her fingers resting lightly on his arm. At her back, she knew eyes were avidly following her and, as she reached the vicinity of the coach, she turned quickly and scanned the house. From every window there was a flurry of retreat. Well, they were no more curious than she. Withering opened the coachdoor and she stepped up and inside. The person seated within was someone known to her.

"I trust you do not mind this rather Gothic way of doing things," said Mrs. Fitzherbert, "but it has been dictated by another."

Lady Augusta assented with a brief movement of her head. "I am delighted to see you, madam, under any circumstances, but I am sorry you will accept my hospitality only so far as the front gate. I do assure you that no unpleasant encounter awaits within."

Mrs. Fitz laughed at this sally, and it was, her hostess realised, the first time she had heard her do it. The sound had a pleasant ring.

"No, I believe the Royal Personage to whom you refer is at this moment in London arguing the question of his allowance with Parliament.

"I have late news of your cousins, however," she continued, "and I fancied I would give myself the pleasure of relating it to you myself."

"I shall be doubly glad to hear it, both for the news and your kindness in transporting it," said Lady Augusta. "What can it be?"

"It seems your Cousin Hermione has at last been located. She and that reprobate had taken a house near Burlington where they lived as husband and wife."

Lady Augusta put a hand to her mouth worriedly. "I distrust the way you say '*as* husband and wife'. Does that mean that he . . . ?"

"I do not know," said Mrs. Fitzherbert. "*She*, at any rate, is of the belief that they are legally married. You will understand my particular interest when I tell you that there is another complication." She smiled ironically. "It seems that his name is not truly Filer, and that he has at least one other wife."

"But that she is safe is the important thing," Lady Augusta said joyfully. "Is she living again at Fogg's Hall?"

"No," the visitor replied, "she is alone, now. He has gone off . . . disappeared . . . and the odd thing is that she prefers to remain where she is. I think she believes he will come back to her."

"But you do not?" asked Lady Augusta.

Mrs. Fitzherbert shook her head sadly. "Not in the honest way she hopes and dreams he will. Poor creature, it is not very much of a life."

"Are their any compensations?" asked Lady Augusta, knowing the conversation was now being conducted on two levels.

"Very few." There was a wealth of experience in the reply. The visitor patted Lady Augusta's hand in a companionable way. "And, now, I must be on my way. I have taken a house in Penzance, perhaps you will call on me one day."

"In Penzance?" asked Lady Augusta, rather dazed.

"I fancied a breath of sea air that carried no old memories upon it."

Lady Augusta, taking her leave, began to climb down from the coach, carefully placing her foot on the step. From within Mrs. Fitzherbert was saying, "Doubtless you will want a word with my coachman before I go off." From without a disturbing and familiar voice said, "If you will give me your hand, milady?"

He was wearing the coachman's cloak and hat, even carrying the whip of the trade, but she had no patience with that.

"Where on earth have you been?" she asked him with a great show of asperity.

He handed up the cape and hat to Withering on the box, then the whip. "You're sure you can manage them?" he asked.

"Right, sir," said Young Withering with a fingertap to his brow. "If need be, I'll just call on the vicar." The coach began to roll.

"Will they be safe in his hands?" Lady Augusta asked anxiously. She knew the condition of country roads.

"It's all right. The coachman and footman are cooling their heels down the road a bit, just by the Merry Maidens."

Lady Augusta and the duke began to walk slowly up the drive toward the house. She saw another flurry of activity at the windows. "You haven't answered my question," she said. "Where *have* you been?"

He looked at her quizzically. "Will it surprise you that I have been trying to make amends for that sorry business in Cheyne?"

She grimaced. "I believe the only one to whom you could make amends would be His Royal Highness."

"No one else," he replied. "I daresay it was a difficult decision, but in retrospect the Prince has decided to see it as a jape which got out of hand." Towans stopped in the drive and said as if in great surprise, "You know, one must admit the chap has a *great* deal of charm." They laughed at this together and continued arm in arm along the drive.

"And, by the way," he asked, "will you marry me? I have every intention of settling down."

"Put so graciously, how could I say no?"

Inside the house Cora ran into the kitchen. "You'll want to lay on tea, Mr. Branston, and some of them lovely scones. We has company, Mr. Branston!"

Lady Barbara, however, was thoroughly confused. Turning away from the window of the sitting room, she said to her sister, "The Duke of Towans is in the drive, Lavvy, and he appears to be kissing Aunt Augusta!"

"I should think so," the countess replied. "I imagine he is going to marry her."

Lady Barbara was quite stupified. "Marry Aunt Augusta? Lavvy, you cannot be serious! Why would he want to do that?"

Lavinia was gentle. "Possibly, my dear, because he loves her."

Barbara was silent for more than a moment as she watched the pair coming up the drive. Then, "There *is* one consolation, at least," she sighed. "I may not marry the man of my first choice, but I surely will have the finest comeout of the season."

Quite late that evening when the lovers were returning from a starlit stroll about the garden, the duke assumed a serious expression. "There is, my own love, one condition I must require of our alliance before we set the date."

"Ah, we have conditions now?" she enquired. "What will be next?"

"I think you will find it only a very small and unimportant concession."

She drew away a little and viewed him suspiciously, but he drew her back into the circle of his arms. "I want you to give up the notion of operating a gambling salon."

Comfortably, she nestled in the crook of his shoulder. "In London, do you mean?" Her casualness was deceptive.

"Yes, of course. In London."

Lady Augusta considered it. It was a small point, after all. She conceded.

There were, God knows, other cities and towns.

If you have enjoyed this book and would like to
receive details of other Walker Regency romances,
please write to:

Regency Editor
Walker and Company
720 Fifth Avenue
New York, N.Y., 10019